CRASH LAND

Doug Johnstone is the author of a number of acclaimed thrillers, including *Gone Again*, *Hit and Run* and, most recently, *The Jump*. He is also a journalist, songwriter and musician, and has a PhD in nuclear physics. He lives in Edinburgh.

www.dougjohnstone.com

also by Doug Johnstone

TOMBSTONING
THE OSSIANS
SMOKEHEADS
HIT AND RUN
GONE AGAIN
THE DEAD BEAT
THE JUMP

Crash Land

DOUG JOHNSTONE

First published in 2016
by Faber & Faber Ltd
Bloomsbury House
74–77 Great Russell Street
London WC1B 3DA

Typeset by Faber & Faber Ltd
Printed and bound by CPI Group (UK) Ltd, Croydon CR0 4YY

A CIP record for this book
is available from the British Library

ISBN 978-0-571-33086-7

2 4 6 8 10 9 7 5 3 1

For Aidan and Amber

We never find what we set our hearts on. We ought to be glad of that.

Beside the Ocean of Time, George Mackay Brown

Author's Note

All events and characters in this book are entirely fictional, but I've tried to stick as closely as possible to the real Orkney. There are a few exceptions for the purpose of dramatic licence. First, there is no bar once you get through security at Kirkwall Airport. Second, while the Tomb of the Eagles is real, I have invented a fictional family who discovered it, rather than the admirable real-life Simisons. I have also changed the proximity of the visitor centre and the nearby farmhouse.

I

Finn watched her come through security. Kirkwall Airport was so small there was nowhere to hide and he spotted her straight away through the Perspex wall, the swing of her hips as she strode towards the X-ray machine. From his stool at the bar he saw her place a holdall in the plastic tray, remove her boots and belt, shrug her jacket off. There was something sexy about it like the start of a striptease, but also wrong, the dehumanising ritual of airport security, as if passengers were being rounded up for internment camps.

With her jacket removed he saw the curve of her body beneath a dark green blouse and black jeans. She waited for the OK from the airport staff and glanced at her bag as it slid into the X-ray. She walked through the metal detector, set the red light flashing and stood to the side, where she was frisked by a female officer then waved on. It was a token effort. What terrorist in their right mind would try anything in Orkney? It was the back of beyond with only internal flights. The chances of trouble were next to zero.

Finn took a sip of his gin and tonic and looked around. He wasn't the only one in the departure lounge to have noticed the woman. Four workies sprawled across plastic chairs drinking pints of Stella stopped their banter to turn and watch her lift her bag from the tray as it came out of the machine. She grabbed her belt and looped it through her jeans then put her boots on. Finn watched the men watching her. There was something obscene about this too, like they were all spying on her getting dressed. It felt abusive somehow.

Finn looked out the window at the runway. He hoped the fog didn't get any worse, he needed to get out of here. Orkney was fine in small doses but he wanted to be back in Dundee for Christmas, where he could clear his head and work on his degree show. Then again, Amy was waiting for him there, and that was a whole other thing.

He could just make out the Loganair twin-prop fuelling on the runway, fog swirling round its nose. The worst place in the world to put an airport, in the lowest hollow on the Mainland where the haar always gathered. A mile down the coast there were probably clear skies swimming with stars.

Finn took another hit from his drink and watched as the woman came in, checked the departures screen, then sat down and fiddled with the strap of her bag, her foot tapping on the scratchy carpet. The workies were looking over and clearly talking about her. Finn saw a Talisman logo on one of the guys' jackets. So they were oil-processing workers from the Flotta terminal, getting the last flight out of Orkney on the Friday before Christmas, heading south to their families.

The biggest of the four guys stood, hitched his jeans and sauntered over to the woman. She was beautiful. Older than Finn, maybe in her early thirties, but with cheekbones and dark eyes that would still look great at fifty. When she saw Oil Guy she rolled those eyes, shifted her body away from him and took a firmer grip of her bag. Before he even reached her she was shaking her head as she looked out the window.

Oil Guy began chatting to her, ignoring the body language, moving into her eyeline. His mates laughed and nudged each other like they were in the playground. Oil Guy sat down next to her and she said something sharp, but he kept on talking with a confident smile. He was over six feet tall with solid biceps squeezed into a tight black T-shirt, a real gym monkey. Buzz cut and work boots. He was probably the same height as Finn but they couldn't have been more different in physique.

The woman shifted her bag and said something else that looked spiky. Oil Guy laughed. She began to stand up but the guy put a hand on her arm. The woman stumbled back in her seat. Finn looked round. The two security officers were chatting at the X-ray machine, turned the other way. The barmaid had disappeared from behind the bar. The Loganair woman at the departure gate was flicking through some paperwork. There was no one else here except Oil Guy's mates.

Finn finished his drink and got up from his bar stool just as the woman yanked her arm from Oil Guy's grip, stood up and swore at him. He smiled like it was a game. She strode over to the bar clutching her holdall in her fist.

'What are you drinking?' she said, looking at Finn's empty glass.

'Gin and tonic.'

'Buy me one. Make it a double.'

Finn turned and saw the barmaid emerging from through the back. He ordered two doubles then looked over his shoulder while she poured them. Oil Guy was heading back to his mates with a walk like a silverback, glaring at Finn.

Finn paid for the drinks and handed one to the woman.

She held up her finger to the barmaid. 'Just a minute.' She

downed her drink and placed it on the bar. 'Same again.' She turned to Finn. 'Thanks, I needed that.'

Finn nodded over his shoulder. 'Was that guy being an arsehole?'

'Nothing I can't handle.'

'What makes you think I'm any better?'

The woman raised her eyebrows and scoped him up and down. 'You look pretty harmless.'

'Thanks.'

'You're welcome.'

Finn stuck out his hand. 'I'm Finn, by the way.'

She shook his hand and put on a mock-serious face, making a joke of the formality.

'I'm Maddie.'

Two more gins arrived and Maddie paid with a twenty. The barmaid stuck it under the UV light then rang it through and handed back the change.

'Cheers,' Maddie said.

Finn clinked glasses and watched as Maddie took a big skelp. The paleness of her neck as she tilted her head back, the way her auburn hair shook when she shivered at the alcohol. Her eyes were very dark brown and she had a sliver of freckles across her nose and cheeks.

She glanced behind Finn at the oil workers, who were staring at them. 'Morons.'

'Want me to get one of the security guys?' Finn said.

Maddie shook her head and a flick of hair went in her eyes. She pulled a red hair tie off her wrist and whipped her hair into a loose bun at the back, exposing more neck.

'It's just guys, you know?'

'I'm a guy.'

'I mean macho bullshit. Some guys act like they're entitled to the world.'

'How do you know I'm not like that?'

'Educated guess.'

'Are your educated guesses always right?'

She laughed. 'Christ, no. I have a terrible record of choosing men.'

'Choosing men?'

'Oh, shut up.'

The buzz from the gin had kicked in and Finn felt a little reckless. He was in an airport drinking and flirting with an attractive woman ten years older than him. It was Friday night and he felt on the edge of something in his mind.

Amy was back in the flat in Dundee, but so what? Things had cooled there so quickly after them hooking up that they felt like an old married couple going through the motions already. The truth was he dreaded going home and sitting in that living room, the same one he'd shared with his mum growing up. All he'd done was replace her after she died with another mother figure. The woman sitting next to him now felt nothing like his mother.

He stole glances at her while they drank. Her skin was smooth except for small creases around the eyes. A sharp nose and small mouth gave her a serious look, but those deep eyes balanced it out. His gaze moved down to her silver necklace, typical Orcadian, interlinked leafing with an aquamarine enamel teardrop set in it.

'My face is up here,' she said, pointing comically at her cheek.

Blood rushed to his face as he shook his head. 'I was looking at your pendant.'

'That's what they all say.'

'From Sheila Fleet, right? Eighteen-inch sterling silver chain, aquamarine stone. I bet you paid seventy-five quid.'

'Are you a salesman?'

Finn shook his head. 'I make jewellery. I could've done you one half the price. Better design too.'

Maddie smiled. It was lopsided, higher on the left than the right, almost a smirk. 'Professionally?'

'Not yet, still studying. Jewellery and metal design. I'm in my final year at Duncan of Jordanstone.'

'Aren't you just the sweetest,' Maddie said. 'What sort of things do you make?'

Finn lifted his rucksack from the floor and pulled out a notebook, handed it over.

She put her gin down and undid the elastic binding, flicked it open. She landed on some sketches he'd done at the Ring of Brodgar a couple of days ago, using the worn curves of the standing stones as templates for a series of brooches. She nodded and flicked through the pages to some rough drawings he'd done at Skara Brae, based on the carved objects there.

'These will be grey onyx,' Finn said. 'Not sure about the settings yet.'

Maddie closed the sketchbook and handed it back. 'So you're a sensitive artistic type.'

Finn shoved it back in his bag. 'I don't know about that.'

'Don't knock it, makes a change.'

Finn nodded at her necklace. 'From the guy who gave you that?'

She frowned.

'Sorry,' Finn said.

Maddie finished her drink. 'Don't be. You've nothing to be sorry about.'

He looked at her left hand. No ring but maybe a mark on the skin where one had been recently. Perhaps she was on the rebound, looking for a little relief after something heavy.

She reached into his open rucksack and pulled something out. 'What's this?'

It was a George Mackay Brown book. He always brought it with him when he came north. She flipped it over to read the back.

'It's my mum's,' Finn said.

'She's a reader, then.'

'She's dead.'

Maddie looked up. 'Sorry.'

She handed the book over and their fingers touched.

'It's fine,' Finn said. He riffled the pages, looked at the crinkled spine. 'She loved this. I'm named after the main character.'

'What's he like?'

Finn smiled. 'A lazy dreamer, kind of.'

'Doesn't sound too bad.'

Finn looked at the departures screen. Their flight was the only one left.

'So what's taking you to Edinburgh?'

Maddie pursed her lips. 'Escape.'

Finn laughed. 'Dramatic.'

Maddie fixed him with a stare. 'Sometimes life is dramatic.' She forced a smile and waved the barmaid over. 'Two more, thanks.' Then to Finn: 'Sorry, take no notice of me.'

'It's impossible not to notice you.' He tried to say it straight, but his bullshit detector made him end in a self-mocking voice.

Maddie laughed. 'Please, you're as bad as those dicks over there.'

Finn looked at the oil workers. They weren't laughing any more, just drinking. He swallowed the last of the gin and picked up his new one.

A voice came over the tannoy.

'We apologise to all passengers on flight BE 6898, but take-off will be delayed by approximately one hour. This is due to inclement weather conditions.'

It was the Loganair woman at the gate who'd said the words into a microphone. There were so few of them in the departure lounge she could've come and told them personally.

'Stupid fog,' Maddie said.

She was looking past the security guards, down the corridor.

'You in a hurry?' Finn said.

'I just need to get away.'

Her grip was hard on the strap of her holdall. Delicate bones, veins tight across the knuckles. She seemed ready to throw a punch.

His phone rang. He pulled it out and checked the screen. Amy. He pressed cancel and put it away.

'No one important?' Maddie said.

He shook his head.

'Well, it looks like we've got an extra hour to burn,' he said. 'Tell me about yourself.'

'Buy me another drink first.'

2

It was nearly two hours before the fog shifted enough for them to board the plane. By that time Finn wasn't sure how much he'd drunk, though they'd settled into a slower pace and switched from doubles to singles.

Maddie went to the toilet before they headed to the gate, taking her bag with her. She hadn't told Finn much about herself. She was originally from Edinburgh but had lived in Orkney for ten years. She'd been with someone until very recently, maybe the reason she was leaving. She didn't have family in Edinburgh any more, and wasn't planning on staying there long. She gave up that personal information with a raised eyebrow and her lopsided smile, so it seemed more like delivering lines than telling the truth.

Finn had spent most of the last two hours talking about himself, his poor little orphan sob story. He wasn't stupid, he knew it played well with women. Brought up in a small two-bedroom flat in Dundee by his mum, Sally, who died two years ago, an aneurysm in the night and she just didn't wake up. His gran, Ingrid, had come down from Orkney to deal with everything and look after Finn. He was just nineteen then, and he and Ingrid struggled, losing a mum and a daughter between them. They were the only family each other had now.

He'd been up for a week staying with her. It was the anniversary of Sally's death and they'd decided to spend it together.

Sally was buried in the graveyard at St Peter's Kirk next to her dad, so the trip was a way for Finn to visit her too.

As a kid he'd spent summers in Orkney, Sally shipping him off during the holidays while she worked a cleaning job and behind the reception desk at the DCA, scraping together enough to pay the mortgage. Finn wondered about that, why Sally never asked Ingrid for help. Sally was artistic, had gone to Dundee to study fine art. When she got pregnant with Finn in her final year, she carried on and passed her degree two days after his due date. Whoever the dad was, he'd never been in the picture, and when Finn got older and asked about him Sally just shrugged and said the two of them didn't need anyone else.

She'd kept on with art for a while, collages and crafty stuff, sculptures of found objects. She did waitressing and cleaning, anything flexible that fitted around childcare. She could've gone back to Orkney, to Ingrid, but she never did. Maybe she saw that as defeat, an admission that she couldn't make it as a grown-up and a parent. Finn would never know. But she was back in Orkney for ever now, and Finn's trips north kept him connected to her.

So he knew Orkney pretty well but not like a local, not like Ingrid, who'd rarely left the islands since she was born. These days she worked part-time at the Tomb of the Eagles, the Stone Age tourist attraction at the tip of South Ronaldsay. It was a couple of miles along from her cottage, as far south as you could get on Orkney before you fell into the sea. It was an amazing place, a chambered cairn full of human remains and eagle bones, and the cliff it was built on was just as dramatic. While Ingrid showed tourists around, Finn would spend the summers helping out and exploring. Then when he was older he borrowed her car and drove around the islands, finding the hidden nooks that tourists never did.

Maddie had said she lived in Stromness, the main town on the West Mainland. Orcadians referred to the main island of Orkney as the Mainland, as opposed to the mainland of Scotland, which they insisted on calling Scotland. Like it was a different country, which of course it was to many of them. Stromness was the second biggest town in Orkney after Kirkwall, which wasn't saying much, precious little to it except a couple of streets, the harbour and two thousand hardy souls. Finn tried to imagine what Maddie did with her time there, what kept her there for ten years. She hadn't said if she had a job or not and he hadn't asked about the man situation, for obvious reasons. But she seemed too big a personality to live in such a sleepy town. She was restless, not someone content to sit around watching daytime television. But then what did he know, he was making assumptions, creating a woman he could fall for in his half-cut mind.

She came back from the toilet and they headed to the gate. The four oil workers were finishing their pints as Finn and Maddie walked past, and one of them grunted in their direction. The big guy she'd knocked back just eyeballed them.

A middle-aged couple were in front of them getting their boarding cards checked. They'd turned up in a fluster just after the delay was announced, complaining in Yorkshire accents about their taxi driver. They relaxed when they realised the plane was late, getting iPads out to play Candy Crush and Sudoku. They had matching fleeces and backpacks, the man placing his hand at the woman's waist now as they went through the gate, guiding her to the runway.

There was a hold-up on the tarmac. A guy in a yellow hi-vis jacket held his hand up for them to stop at the steps of the plane. He spoke into a radio then angled his head to listen to the reply. The evening was blowy but Finn felt hemmed in, the fog damp on his face. They were only a few hundred yards from the sea, over to the north behind the plane, but he couldn't see much past the tail of the aircraft. He loved flying on these little twin-props, the informality so different from the herding of package holidays. With eight passengers in a twenty-eight-seater there would be plenty of room to spread out. He and Maddie could sit together despite their allocated seats being six rows apart, no one cared about that up here.

'What now?' Maddie said to Hi-Vis, then looked behind her.

Finn followed her gaze and saw the oil workers coming out of the terminal. He chewed the inside of his cheek.

'Come on, mate.' It was the tallest oil worker, the knock-back guy, approaching Hi-Vis. 'We're freezing our tits off here.'

The guy turned away and spoke into the radio. Finn thought he heard something like 'fuel cap'. He imagined a car's fuel cap dangling loose as it drove away from a petrol station. Ridiculous, this was a small flight but it had all the same safety regulations as bigger planes.

Maddie looked past the oil workers, at the terminal. Hi-Vis gave them the all clear and the middle-aged couple started up the steps. Maddie put her holdall down on the tarmac, opened it and rummaged inside. She lifted her head and spoke to the oil workers.

'On you go.'

They bustled up the stairs.

'Everything OK?' Finn said.

'Just pretending. Let those pricks go in front so we don't end up sitting next to them.' She zipped up the holdall, slung it over her shoulder and stood up. 'Let's get out of here.'

3

They sat near the back like a childish conspiracy, the bad kids on the school bus. The middle-aged couple were in the front row like swots, the oil workers spread across rows E and F. The weekend before Christmas, the last flight off the island, and the alcohol made Finn feel loose and edgy. Charlotte the stewardess had greeted them as they boarded. She was about the same age as Finn, with hipster glasses, braided blonde hair and no make-up, and she somehow managed to make the Loganair purple and blue uniform seem cool.

Maddie sat at the window with her bag under the seat in front. Finn offered to throw it into the overhead locker with his rucksack but she shook her head. There was something about her Finn couldn't fathom, her mood could be thrown between sunshine and darkness in a few moments. A minute ago she'd giggled with him about the hole in the back of Charlotte's tights, but now she stared out the window at the wisps of fog feathering the plane's wings.

Finn sat in the seat next to her. 'Nervous flyer?'

'Sometimes.'

He put his hand on hers. 'I'll take care of you.'

He made a goofy face, tried to undermine his cheesy line again, but Maddie didn't go along with it this time.

'You're a sweet boy.'

'I'm twenty-one.'

'Exactly.'

He play-punched her arm. 'I'm a man.'

She punched him back. 'Ug, me big man, get woman.'

'Is that what you think I'm trying to do?'

She laughed. 'We both know what's going on.'

Finn shook his head. 'I don't.'

'Yes, you do.'

Engine noise flooded the cabin, overhead lights flickering for a moment. Charlotte pulled the collapsible steps up from the doorway into the cabin and folded them away behind her seat, then sealed the hatch. A voice came over the intercom but the only thing Finn made out over the propeller noise was 'seventeen thousand feet'. Charlotte stood at the front of the plane doing the actions, emergency exits here and here, oxygen masks and life jackets. She blew into the tube to reinflate the life jacket. What was the point of that? If you crashed in the sea up here you'd freeze to death in seconds, no time to puff up your life jacket.

'What are your plans when we land?' he said to Maddie.

'I might just hop on another plane.'

'You really are escaping.'

'You have no idea.'

'Then tell me.'

She touched his hand on the armrest. 'Maybe when I get to know you better.'

'So you do want to get to know me better.'

'Can you say anything without it sounding like a come-on?'

'I can't help it, I'm half drunk on a plane with a mysterious, beautiful woman.'

'Mysterious,' Maddie said. 'I like that.'

'Don't forget beautiful.'

Maddie smiled. 'What are your plans when we hit Edinburgh?'

'Train to Dundee.'

'You don't look too happy about it.'

'Let's talk about something else.'

'I'm not the only one who's mysterious.'

She looked out the window again. Finn was sure there was something here. He'd always been a serial monogamist, devoting himself to a girl then, when it ended, falling straight into another relationship. But this was different with Maddie, this was a game and he didn't know the rules. Smoke and mirrors, innuendo and suggestion. He wasn't sure of anything.

And then there was Amy. He'd never been unfaithful before, always thought he couldn't deceive a girlfriend. Yet here he was with someone else, hardly giving Amy a thought. But there was no excitement back home, it was comfortable and boring for both of them. They were only still together because of inertia, because neither of them had the courage to admit they were sleepwalking through it. He'd needed someone reliable after his mum died, a rock to be anchored to, and Amy had been that. If he was honest, it was disgraceful the way he'd let it drift this far, the way they both had.

Charlotte walked down the cabin checking seatbelts. She looked put out that she had to walk to the back to check on Finn and Maddie, but she didn't say anything.

Maddie was still gazing out the window, her hand fiddling with the pendant at her throat.

Finn glanced past her. 'Is the fog getting worse again?' He had to raise his voice over the propeller noise shuddering the plane.

'Do you really make jewellery?' she said.

'Yeah.'

'Will you make something for me?'

'I'd love to.'

'Not a freebie, I can pay.'

Finn shook his head. 'It would be an honour to create something for such a beautiful neck.'

Maddie mimed sticking her fingers down her throat.

'You don't have much experience with women, do you?'

'This is my tactic, make an ass of myself then take the piss out of myself for it.'

'Don't, you sound like all the rest.'

'Who?'

'Players,' Maddie said. 'Guys who think they're it. Pulling techniques and strategies, targeting women with low self-esteem, conquering the opposite sex.'

'I'm not like that.'

'Good.'

The plane taxied across the airfield, engines racing. One of the oil workers unbuckled and headed for the toilet but Charlotte put out a firm hand and made him get back in his seat. His mates laughed as he squirmed.

Finn felt a buzz and pulled his phone out of his pocket. Amy again. He sucked on the tip of his tongue and stared at her name on the screen. There was a feature on his phone where you could add a picture to incoming calls, but he'd never got round to it. Maybe if Amy's face had popped up he would've felt worse about what he was doing. Thinking of doing. He pressed cancel.

'Should be on airplane mode,' Maddie said.

'Have you ever heard of a plane crashing because someone kept a phone on?'

'And you're the expert.'

'Fair enough.'

'Give it here, while you've got it out,' she said, taking the phone from him. She got her own phone out and punched his number into her contacts.

Finn smiled. 'Why do you want my number?'

She handed it back. 'You never know.'

The plane turned and stopped at the end of the runway. Finn knew from previous flights that they were next to the sea now, but he couldn't see anything in the haar.

The engines roared and he felt the thrust of the plane as it began take-off. Maddie's hand found his and squeezed at his knuckle. He placed his other hand on top but the look in her eyes wasn't afraid, just relieved to be going.

The rumble of the wheels on tarmac grew louder then stopped as the plane lifted into the air, beads of wet fog flung from the wing, smearing across the window like tears. The cabin juddered and rolled as a crosswind hit, and Finn saw the wing bend. The flexibility of aeroplanes always amazed him, giant metal constructions that submitted to the elements, moved with the weather, allowing them to slip through unmolested.

They were pushed back in their seats now, the cabin at a steep angle as the pilot climbed to get above the fog. Finn imagined being in the cockpit in this weather, flying blind, just the radar and a voice from the tower to reassure you that there was nothing looming in the darkness.

He remembered a thing he'd done with his mum when he

was about six years old. She'd told him to walk as far as possible along the pavement with his eyes closed. He'd lasted twenty steps before the tension became unbearable. Even though there was no one about and the path was flat and straight he still couldn't go on without knowing what was ahead. Maybe he just wasn't a risk taker. Sally had laughed then tried it herself and got five times further than him. 'Maybe you'll do better as you get older,' she said. 'There's less to surprise you when you've been around for a while.'

The angle of the cabin levelled out. The seatbelt sign went off and he felt pressure on his bladder, as if his body had been waiting for the signal.

'I'm just going to the toilet,' he said.

Maddie turned from the window and smiled. 'Hurry back.'

4

He pulled the folding door closed and slid the lock over. His phone rang. He hadn't put it on airplane mode. He pulled it out of his pocket. Amy.

He answered. 'Hi, honey.'

'I've been trying to get you.'

He didn't feel anything at the sound of her voice and he hated himself for that. 'Sorry, I had it on silent.'

'You OK?'

'Fine.'

'You sound different, that's all. I was worried, with the anniversary of your mum and everything.'

He cared about her of course, but it wasn't love, there was no spark. He would have to end it. It didn't matter if anything happened with Maddie, but in the hours he'd spent with her he'd felt more alive than he had done in the last year with Amy. That wasn't right. But he couldn't do it over the phone, that was gutless. When he got back to Dundee he would speak to her, make her see that they had drifted apart and it was over.

'I'm OK,' he said.

'I saw that your weather wasn't great.'

'Fog delayed us for a couple of hours but we're off now.'

'You're on your phone on the plane?'

Finn looked at himself in the toilet mirror. The gin buzz was ebbing away but there was still a fuzzy edge to his reflection, a glow in his eyes. He wondered what Maddie made of him at the airport bar. An easy pick-up, a little bit of fun on the rebound? Or just a safe option compared to the meatheads hassling her?

'We're still on the runway,' he said.

'You'd better get off the phone.'

'Sure.'

'Finn?' There was a tremble in her voice.

'Yeah?'

'Stay safe. I love you.'

He paused, just a beat. 'I love you, too.'

He ended the call. He hadn't thought of himself as deceitful, but here he was. He gripped the sink and looked in the mirror.

He turned and began to piss. The plane lurched and urine splashed round the seat and on to the floor. He put a hand against the mirror to steady himself. He finished and zipped up, pulled out some toilet paper and wiped the seat, then washed his hands. There was a smudge on the mirror where his hand had been. The way he was standing it was right in the middle of his forehead, a smear across his mind.

He left the toilet and stopped.

Oil Guy was sitting in Finn's seat. He was leaning into Maddie, his hand on her arm, speaking under his breath. Maddie tried to pull away, her body squeezed against the window. He stroked her cheek and she squirmed.

'Excuse me,' Finn said.

The guy glanced round, hardly taking notice.

'Fuck off, prick.'

'You're in my seat.'

A wobble in the cabin made Finn place his hand on the headrest, a few inches from the guy's head.

Oil Guy turned, still holding Maddie's arm.

'Sit somewhere else.'

'That's my seat.'

'We're busy.'

Finn looked round the cabin. The other three oil workers were smiling at him. The middle-aged couple were oblivious up the front, chatting to Charlotte, who was leaning over their seats.

'I don't think she wants to speak to you,' Finn said.

'It's not about what she wants, it's what she needs. And I know what she needs.'

'That hurts,' Maddie said. She tried to pull away but he held firm. Her skin where he gripped it was red.

'Get your hands off her,' Finn said.

Oil Guy took him in. 'It's a bit late to grow bollocks.'

'Just leave us alone.'

'Or what?'

'I'll make you.'

Oil Guy laughed and turned to Maddie. 'Where did you find this guy?'

'He's a better man than you,' Maddie said.

The guy shook his head. 'If you think that, you've never been with a real man.'

'Just leave,' Finn said.

'Make me.'

Finn put everything into it as he swung his fist at Oil Guy's head, catching him high on the side of the cheek. The guy flinched but not much, then thrust his elbow into Finn's gut, knocking the air out of him. Finn doubled over as the guy came out of his seat and launched at him, and the two of them tumbled into the aisle, bouncing off seats. The guy got an arm clear and swung a heavy punch at Finn's face, catching his mouth, and Finn felt his jaw crack. He tried to get his arms out but the guy had him in a bear hug, squeezing his ribs. Finn jerked a knee up and caught the guy in the bollocks, and he loosened his grip. Finn brought both fists down on the back of the guy's head but he just looked up and headbutted Finn in the face. There was a burst of blood from his nose and a metal taste in his mouth as his eyes watered. Through the tears Finn could see Maddie grabbing at the guy, trying to pull him off, and beyond that he could see the other oil workers clambering out of their seats and down the cabin. Charlotte and a guy in uniform who must've been the co-pilot were pushing past them as the cabin swayed through another bubble of turbulence.

Finn threw his fist at Oil Guy's stomach. The hit landed but didn't have much effect and the guy grabbed Finn's hair and pulled his head downwards, kicking at Finn's legs at the same time. Finn lost balance and toppled to the floor, then felt the weight of the guy on top of him. He raised his arms as blows rained down on his chest and head. Finn lashed out when he could, catching the guy on the chin with one punch, but it was one hit against a flood sweeping over him. Three more blows to his stomach left him heaving for breath, then Oil Guy landed another one on his face and Finn felt a tooth loosen.

He opened his eyes to see the co-pilot and Maddie hauling at Oil Guy, pulling him away. The guy got in a couple of kicks as he was dragged off, one on the side of Finn's knee that sent pain knifing up his leg.

The co-pilot pushed the guy back into a seat then pulled out plastic restraints and slipped them on his wrists. Before he could complain the co-pilot knelt down and secured his ankles together with more plastic ties.

'What the fuck?' Oil Guy said.

'I'm performing a citizen's arrest,' the co-pilot said, 'under the Civil Aviation Act.'

'He started it.'

Charlotte and Maddie put hands out to help Finn up. There was pain in his knee, his mouth, his nose. He gasped air into his lungs but couldn't speak. He slumped into a seat then felt Charlotte pop restraints over his wrists and tighten them. He looked at her as she knelt and did his ankles.

'What are you doing?' he said.

'I'm performing a citizen's arrest under the Civil Aviation Act,' she said.

Maddie touched Charlotte on the shoulder.

'Get your hand off me, miss, unless you want to be arrested as well.'

Maddie stared. 'The other guy started it, he assaulted me. Finn was trying to help.'

'I saw this gentleman throw the first punch,' Charlotte said.

'That's right,' said Oil Guy, leaning forward in his seat. 'Let me out of these.'

'This is all a misunderstanding,' Finn said. 'Let me go and I won't be any trouble.'

'We'll let the police decide,' the co-pilot said.

Oil Guy looked worried. 'There's no need for that.'

His friends crowded round the co-pilot, who spoke over them.

'Charlotte, go tell the captain what's happened.'

Charlotte strode up the aisle past the Yorkshire couple, who had left their seats to watch. She knocked and ducked into the cockpit. Finn saw banks of controls, the epaulettes on the pilot's shoulder, blackness outside the glass.

'This is bullshit,' Oil Guy said. 'You don't have the authority for this.'

The co-pilot stuck his chin out. 'I absolutely do have the authority.'

One of the oil worker's pals spoke up. 'We don't want any trouble.'

'Try telling him that,' the co-pilot said.

'This is ridiculous,' Maddie said.

The co-pilot folded his arms. 'You think so? They've compromised safety on an aircraft in flight.'

Charlotte came back down the aisle. 'Everyone back in your seats, please.'

Maddie stared at her. 'Why?'

'Just get back in your seat, miss.'

'I want to know what's going on.'

There was a crackle of static and a voice came over the speaker. The cabin shuddered and everyone braced.

'This is the captain. I've spoken to authorities on the ground about the situation on board, and we have decided to return to Kirkwall Airport to ensure everyone's safety and security.'

'Fuck's sake,' Oil Guy said.

The captain was still talking. 'Please return to your seats immediately and fasten your seatbelts in preparation for landing.'

'This is crazy,' Finn said. 'There's no need to go back.'

The co-pilot looked at him. 'Standard procedure in the event of a disturbance on board.'

Maddie shook her head. 'We can't go back.'

Charlotte put a hand out to her. 'Please return to your seat.'

'No,' Maddie said.

The oil workers were standing behind her, angry.

'We've got folk to get home to,' one of them said. 'If we go back to Kirkwall, Christ knows when we'll get off that rock.'

The co-pilot shrugged. 'Take it up with your friend.' He turned to Finn. 'And him. It's their fault.'

Maddie pushed past Charlotte and the oil workers and ran towards the cockpit.

'Miss, return to your seat immediately,' Charlotte said.

'I'm not going back,' Maddie said.

The plane was already banking, shifting their centre of gravity. Finn wondered how far they'd got from Orkney, probably only just over the Pentland Firth.

Maddie was already at the cockpit door. She pushed it open and stepped inside as the pilot turned with a surprised look. Charlotte and the co-pilot ran up the aisle but Maddie spotted them and slammed the cockpit door. The co-pilot grabbed the handle and pushed but the door didn't budge.

The plane took another wobble. They were at a steep angle, the oil workers leaning to remain upright against the shift. Finn looked out the window at the wing, light blinking, rain streaming over the metal curve, haar swirling.

The co-pilot and Charlotte hammered on the door and shouted.

The plane lurched in the same direction as the bank, throwing the oil workers into seats. Finn felt his armrest digging into his side. He tugged at his restraints but they stayed tight.

The co-pilot pushed his shoulder against the cockpit door

and it fell open. The engine roared in the cabin as Charlotte and the co-pilot shouted at Maddie, who had her hands on the pilot's arm.

The co-pilot got her in an arm lock, dragged her out of the cockpit and threw her into a seat in the front row. He held her there, standing to the side to avoid her kicking legs as she struggled. He barked something to Charlotte, who reached into a compartment next to the food trolley and pulled out more restraints.

But before she could hand them over to the co-pilot the cabin lurched again, the nose of the plane plunging downwards, throwing Charlotte back against the cockpit door and making the co-pilot stumble. Finn caught the panicked look in his eyes. The plane's nose tipped up, then two more jolts tilted them all to the left.

The co-pilot and Charlotte crawled over and pulled themselves into flip-down crew seats, fumbling with seatbelts. Maddie did the same, scrambling for her belt.

Finn fumbled for his own and pulled it tight as the plane lunged forward again, throwing him into the seat in front, scudding his head off the headrest.

Oil Guy turned and looked at him with narrow eyes.

There was a metallic crack as the plane reeled left then right, then pitched downwards. Finn looked out the window and thought he saw lights. Landing lights or houses?

The screech of landing gear was suddenly all around but it didn't sound right, too loud and grating. They surely couldn't land the plane at this angle. The cabin pitched and yawed and Finn felt sick.

Then they hit the ground.

A scream of metal ripped in Finn's ears as his knees were thrown into his chest. He looked up and the cabin had been severed into two pieces, split a few rows in front, both halves hurtling at Christ knows what speed, cold air filling the space, the excruciating grind of metal on metal, steel on tarmac. Two of the oil workers were thrown out of their seats and smashed down into the aisle, then another thrash and lurch and Finn's head smacked into his seat. Something moved out the window. It was the wing, broken free, bouncing up into the air off the tarmac, flipping over through fog then slicing down into the front half of the cabin, the broken propellers and thick cylinder of the engine landing on the front row where the couple were. Dust and dirt spewed everywhere, the cabin shredding itself along the ground, the front half spinning sideways.

The severed wing was on fire, flames leaping through the seats. The overhead lockers were open and bags flew out. Finn tried to scream but couldn't get air into his lungs as the plane hammered along the runway, throwing debris and seats up from the front so that he had to duck out of the way.

He lifted his head and saw the front part of the plane fifty yards away and still moving, flames licking the cockpit. They were losing momentum as they scraped along the runway. Finn saw the airport building up to the left, which meant they were skidding towards the perimeter fence and the sea.

Their half of the fuselage jerked upwards at the back before crashing down, unhinging the row of seats Finn was in, flipping him towards the rear of the cabin where his skull connected with the wall, bursts of purple and red in his vision, pain screaming through him until his body gave up to the blackness.

5

The fumes hit him first and he gagged. It felt like he was breathing petrol. He coughed then puked down himself. Pain swarmed through him, the back of his head, his ribs on the left-hand side, his knee. Something felt very wrong with his right hand. He tried to breathe but pain sliced across his chest as his lungs expanded. He spat sick out of his mouth and opened his eyes.

He was still strapped in his seat, which was now on the floor at the back of the aisle, pushed up against the toilet wall. In the rows in front of him only half the seats were still there, the rest pitched upside down on top of others or presumably somewhere outside the cabin.

Two of the oil workers were on the floor further up the aisle, one with a seat and a small case on top of him. The guy he'd fought with was in his seat a couple of rows in front, slumped over with his head to the side.

Where the fuselage had ripped in two, ragged metal and plastic edges were exposed, torn fabric flapping in the breeze. The stench of fuel was everywhere as Finn tried moving his head.

He could see the front half of the plane not too far away, as if the two pieces had tried their best not to be parted. The front seats were crushed by the engine. The fire there had gone out, leaving rows of scorched headrests. Beyond that the co-pilot and Charlotte were still strapped in, seemingly unconscious. Behind them, the cockpit door was closed. He couldn't see Maddie. Her seat was still bolted in place, but he couldn't see her head. Maybe she was unconscious, flopped to the side.

Between the two parts of the plane was grey tarmac. Beyond that was rough grass, tussocks of sandy gorse. They'd managed to stay on the runway, but he could hear waves so they must be close to the sea.

Jesus, the pain. He looked at his right hand. The two smallest fingers were pointing in the wrong direction, at a right angle to the knuckle, which had flattened. He tried to flex it and felt bone grind under the skin, a shard of pain up his arm.

He put his head back on the seat. His wrists and ankles were still bound. He felt dizzy, the fumes taking over. He closed his eyes and tried not to be sick again, concentrated on breathing.

Sirens. They were coming. Everything was going to be OK.

He heard movement in the cabin. His head was spinning as he drifted close to passing out, an awful kind of vertigo, control of his mind slipping away.

He opened his eyes and saw Maddie.

She stepped down the aisle towards him, rubbing her eye. She was alive and she was coming for him.

'Are you OK?' she said.

Finn nodded.

She knelt down.

Finn looked at his right hand and she followed his gaze. 'Christ, your fingers.'

'It's not too bad.'

'I'm so sorry.'

Finn shook his head, his skull thudding. 'It's not your fault, it's mine.'

She put a finger to his lips, then leaned in and kissed him.

The sirens were getting louder.

Maddie pulled away and looked around, then out through the gaping hole at the front of the cabin. She shook her head.

'I can't do this,' she said under her breath.

She reached under the seat to Finn's left and pulled out her holdall, the one she'd stowed. She clutched it in both hands and looked at him.

'I have to go.'

She turned and walked down the aisle then stepped out the tattered front of the cabin.

The sirens were all around now and Finn saw flashing lights out the window.

Maddie looked back at him then disappeared into the haar.

6

Fingers touched his neck and he thought of her.

He opened his eyes and saw a middle-aged paramedic with a grey beard and wild hair.

'What's your name?'

'Finn.'

'How do you feel, Finn?'

'Fucked.'

'Well, you've been in a plane crash, that's to be expected. Where does it hurt?'

Finn took shallow breaths. 'The left side of my chest. The back of my head. My hand.'

The paramedic looked at Finn's hands and saw the restraints.

'I can explain,' Finn said.

The paramedic shook his head. 'I'm not interested. Save your strength, you're going to need it.'

'It wasn't my fault.'

The paramedic rooted through a kit bag on the floor and pulled out a scalpel.

'We can't treat you with these things on,' he said, slicing the plastic at Finn's wrists and ankles. 'Don't run off, now.'

Finn pictured Maddie out there in the darkness, stumbling through the grass towards the sea.

'Jesus.' It was a woman's voice coming from behind the paramedic.

'I know.' The paramedic put the scalpel back in the bag and took out a torch, shone it in Finn's eyes.

'Has anyone declared a major incident yet?' the woman said.

'Don't think so,' the paramedic said.

'I'll do it now.'

The paramedic pushed Finn's eyelids up and examined him. 'Signs of concussion.'

'I feel sick.'

'Don't puke, I just got this uniform cleaned.'

'I might pass out.'

The paramedic looked at him. 'Just don't die. I hate it when folk die.'

He unfolded a silver blanket from the bag and draped it over Finn, tucking it in. 'We'll look at your chest and hand in a bit, probably just broken bones. You'll need to rest, with the concussion. Someone will be with you in a minute to take you to the ambulance. I need to check on the others.'

He stepped towards Oil Guy, saw the restraints on his hands and feet. He turned to Finn. 'A friend of yours?'

'No,' Finn said.

He looked round. The woman's voice belonged to a young, short police officer in a puffy winter jacket. She was at the torn edge of the fuselage talking on the phone, a look on her face that said this was the worst shitstorm she'd ever seen.

A matronly paramedic was tending to one of the oil workers on the floor. She pulled up an eyelid and shook her head. 'No pulse, suspected broken neck.' She moved to the other guy, who was face down on the floor, and tried to turn his body but he wouldn't budge. She checked underneath him then jerked upright. She lifted his T-shirt to reveal a jagged metal spike sticking through the skin at the base of his spine. It was the frame of a seat. It had gone right through him. The paramedic lowered the T-shirt and felt the man's neck, then caught the police officer's attention.

Finn felt the cabin swim and closed his eyes.

The paramedic with the beard spoke to his colleague.

'What have you got, Eilidh?'

'Two dead.'

'This guy's unconscious but in a bad way. Let's move him first, then broken bones over there.'

Finn tried to add it up. Him and Maddie, the four oil workers, the Yorkshire couple. Eight passengers. The stewardess, pilot and co-pilot meant eleven in total. Two dead on the floor. The couple in the front row were surely dead too, crushed by the engine. The co-pilot and stewardess still looked alive at the front. He hadn't seen the pilot. Wait, where was the fourth oil worker?

And Maddie.

Every time he breathed his ribcage screamed at him. He breathed out the right side of his mouth, as if that would make a difference. His hand throbbed. He opened his eyes and Oil Guy was being lifted away on a stretcher. The police officer came over and knelt down next to him.

'Can you walk?'

'I don't know.'

'Let's try.'

She put a hand under his arm and he tried to push out of the seat, but the pressure on his right hand sent pain shuddering through him.

'Shit.'

'Take it easy,' she said. 'The medical guys better deal with you, that's their job.'

'Sure.'

'What's your name?'

'Finn.'

'OK, Finn, I'm Detective Inspector Linklater. Morna. What can you tell me about what happened?'

Finn looked at her. A few years older than him, tight ponytail and broad nose, small mouth and Orkney accent. Local girl done good.

'I'm not sure,' he said.

'We got a call from the airport saying there was an incident on the flight and it was turning back.' She lifted the cut restraints from the cabin floor. 'I just saw Magnus cutting these off you and the other guy. Want to explain?'

'I feel dizzy,' Finn said. 'I need painkillers.'

'Aye, you'll get painkillers.'

'I'm going to be sick.'

Linklater stepped back as Finn puked on the floor. He closed his eyes and heard voices. The two paramedics were back.

'Can you hear me?' Magnus said.

Finn nodded and breathed out, all he could manage.

'Can you walk,' Eilidh said, 'or do you need the stretcher?'

He felt his mind dissolving into the wintry air, merging with the whirl of the wind, the sound of the sea, the earth spinning.

'Stretcher,' he said, then he passed out.

7

He felt himself getting bumped into the ambulance. He tried to sit up but the ribs on his left side screamed. To his right was Oil Guy on a stretcher, attached to a heart monitor and oxygen mask, cuts to his scalp and face. Finn looked out the open ambulance door and saw a body covered in a sheet on the airstrip a hundred feet from the wreckage. The fourth oil worker.

A smirr of rain came swirling into the ambulance, adding a wet sheen to the blanket on his lap and the instruments lined along the side.

The last time he'd seen a dead body was when he found his mum. He'd slept late, been out for a few drinks at the DCA with some students from the year above. He was surprised that Sally hadn't woken him with her banging around in the flat like she usually did when he was hungover. Not that she disapproved particularly, she was partial to a few glasses of wine most nights, but she didn't make allowances for him in that state either, and usually she could be relied on to hoover outside his door around ten or eleven, or clatter dishes and pans into cupboards and drawers from the dishwasher.

So he was surprised when he surfaced at noon and the flat was silent. Maybe she'd gone to the shops. It was a Sunday and she wasn't working. He got up and wandered through to the small kitchen, stuck the kettle on. He noticed it was cold, no residual heat from being on earlier in the morning. The sun was low in the sky, a sharp, cloudless winter day, sunlight glinting off the Tay out the window, sandbanks splitting the surface at low tide, the rail bridge curving over to Fife in the distance.

He stood looking out the window as the kettle filled the room with noise. When it clicked off he went to the cupboard to get a mug and noticed it was half empty. He opened the dishwasher. It hadn't been emptied. He frowned and stepped into the hall.

'Mum?'

He walked to her closed bedroom door, angled his ear towards it.

'Mum?'

Just the creak of a floorboard under his feet.

He turned the handle and opened the door.

She was in bed and he knew right away she was dead. Something about the lack of tension in her skin, the stillness of her, felt completely different to sleep.

He shuffled to her and reached out a hand, touched her cold cheek and kept it there for a long time, staring at her face. Eventually he lowered his hand and backed out the room, his arms hanging useless at his sides, staring at the carpet under his bare feet.

When the ambulance came they confirmed what he already knew. He rode with her to hospital, though he couldn't see the point. Weren't hospitals for the living? But they said they needed to do a post-mortem, make it official. After she was taken away he had to get a taxi back from Ninewells. He put off calling Ingrid for three hours, wanted it to be just his thing for a little longer.

Two days later someone from Ninewells called and gave a

fancy name to Sally's death. A cerebral aneurysm had ruptured, causing a subarachnoid haemorrhage, leading to a massive stroke and brain death. It would've been painless, the woman said down the line, as if it mattered. Maybe it did.

By then Ingrid was with him in Dundee, busying herself around the flat, talking to funeral directors, emptying the dishwasher. The next part of Finn's life had begun, without anyone asking him if he wanted the last part to end.

Looking out the ambulance into the gloom now, he saw a crowd of emergency vehicles beyond the body on the tarmac. Two fire engines were next to the front half of the severed plane, firefighters in clumpy boots and bulky uniforms stamping around. An ambulance and three police cars were parked in between, a couple of guys in uniforms placing cones around the area, unwrapping that yellow tape they used.

Finn looked at the plane. One wing was still attached to the fuselage, but the tip was missing. It looked like a giant injured bird. The rear of the aircraft was relatively intact compared to the front half. The cockpit had concertinaed, crumpled into a snubbed nose, glass missing from the windows. There was a smattering of debris around it. The right engine and wing sat jutting out of the cabin just behind the cockpit, reminding Finn of the metal spike sticking out of the guy's back. His stomach tightened and he struggled to breathe. He put his head down on the stretcher and heard voices outside the ambulance.

'Seven confirmed dead,' Magnus said.

'Christ, we can't handle this,' Linklater said. It sounded like she was close to tears.

'You'll be all right, Morna, just follow procedure.'

'What's the procedure for this?'

Finn imagined Magnus putting a comforting arm around her. Orkney was such a small place, everyone knew each other.

'Do you want us to move the bodies?' Magnus said.

'Wait for forensics. I've called for help from down south. God knows when they'll get here.'

'Can they even land with all this here?'

'They're coming by helicopter. Air and sea rescue are helping.'

'I'll get these two to hospital,' Magnus said. 'Eilidh's already headed to the Balfour with the stewardess in the other ambulance.'

There was a moment's silence between them, just the thrum of machines and the ambulance engine ticking over.

'Three injured?' Linklater said.

'Yes.'

'And seven dead?'

'That's right.'

'Christ,' Linklater said. 'That means someone's missing.'

8

'I won't lie to you, this is going to hurt.'

The badge on her white coat said 'Dr Flett'.

Finn felt a jab as she injected a large amount of liquid into the side of his hand from a big syringe. The liquid went in and his skin stretched tight and bulged like something out of a horror film. Finn imagined the skin rupturing and spraying blood all over the treatment room.

'That wasn't so bad,' he said.

The woman smiled. She was early forties, about the age Sally would've been if she were still around. Strawberry-blonde hair cut into a short bob, green eyes.

'I didn't mean that,' she said. 'That was just the painkiller and local anaesthetic. We need to wait a couple of minutes for you to lose feeling in your hand, then I'll reset the fingers.'

'Reset them?'

She nodded at the X-ray on the backlit screen. A close-up of Finn's hand, two rogue fingers off at a tangent to the rest.

'The knuckle is crushed, the bones in the fingers are fractured and twisted. If I don't reset them they'll fuse squint and you might lose the use of them altogether.'

'Right.'

'It's called a boxer's fracture, although the gloves normally protect real boxers. Mostly we see it in pub fights. Have you been punching someone?'

Finn didn't speak.

'It's none of my business,' Flett said. 'I'm sure the police will talk to you.'

She tapped the side of his hand and wiggled his pinkie finger. Pain shot up his arm and he flinched.

'I guess you can feel that.'

'Yes.'

'Give it another minute.'

She got up and swished away through the blue plastic curtain around the booth. Finn looked round. X-ray display, treatment table covered in a plastic sheet, low shelves stuffed with medical supplies and paperwork. An empty stand for holding drips lurked in the corner.

The ambulance had delivered him to A & E at the Balfour Hospital on the southern outskirts of Kirkwall. It was little more than a pebbledashed hut down a side alley, tagged on to the sprawl of low concrete buildings that made up the overcrowded hospital, skulking in a residential area. Cars were parked all over and the ambulance had to squeeze past them before doing a five-point turn at a dead end so it was pointing the right way to get out again.

Finn was able to walk to the waiting room, which was an improvement. The A & E team took Oil Guy first, wheeled him through to a consultation room deeper in the building. Finn wondered if he was OK. He thought about Charlotte too, the stewardess. Were her injuries serious? The pilot and co-pilot were dead. He wondered if Charlotte knew them well. Maybe she had a thing going with one of them. Maybe she was heartbroken.

Finn prodded at the bulbous skin of his hand. He flicked at

his pinkie and was surprised that it didn't hurt.

The curtain was swept back and Dr Flett came in. She was wearing boot-cut jeans with Nike trainers, a tight purple T-shirt under her open doctor's coat. She was someone's mum, probably, someone's daughter. She fitted into life here on the island and was just doing her job. Finn wondered if she knew any of the dead passengers and crew. Did she realise the extent of what had happened? When word got out his life would be unbearable.

He thought about Maddie.

'OK,' Flett said, gripping his hand. 'You might want to look away.'

Her head was bowed as she concentrated on his fingers. Finn stared at the swirl of her hair, the pattern of follicles, the individual strands. He thought about how many hundreds of thousands of hairs were there. He wondered how much morphine she'd injected into him. He felt the bones in his knuckle crunch and grind against each other, unnatural, like the devil messing with his body. He felt the fingers being twisted into line with the rest of his hand, heard a pop as a bone went back into the joint, then more grinding as Flett jiggled the bones into place, gripping and twisting, bending and massaging. The colour drained from his face. He put out his other hand to steady himself, then his body slumped back on the treatment table, plastic headrest against his scalp, the reassurance of it, something where it was supposed to be.

'You OK?' Flett said.

Finn managed a small nod with his eyes closed.

'I just need to splint it,' Flett said.

Something cold touched the outside of his hand. He opened

his eyes and saw her strapping a metal splint to his smallest finger, along the outside of the palm. Then she taped his two injured fingers together with the middle one.

'This provides support to the two broken ones,' Flett said. 'We call it buddy strapping, attaching the broken fingers to a healthy one.'

Finn thought about that.

Flett moved the hand around, examining her work.

'That'll do.' She nodded at the X-ray display, which had a second image, the left side of Finn's ribcage. A hairline crack in the bone below the nipple. 'Shame we can't do the same for your rib.'

'So what can you do?' Finn said.

Flett shoved a hand into the pocket of her coat, pulled out a box of pills and placed them in Finn's lap.

'Take two whenever you need, no more than eight in twenty-four hours. They're morphine, pretty strong, so they might make you tired or sick. Don't drive or operate machinery, all the usual.'

'OK.'

Flett stood up and put on a smile. 'You're very lucky, I hope you appreciate that.'

'I do.'

She pulled the X-rays from the light box, switched it off and the room went gloomy. 'We'll keep you in overnight for the head knock. Just to watch for complications from concussion.'

'I can go home in the morning?'

Flett looked at him. 'That depends on the police.' She had a hand on the curtain, pulling it back. 'Good luck, I think you're going to need it.'

9

The door of his hospital room opened and Ingrid walked in.

'My boy.' She put her hands to her face then stretched them towards him as she came to the bed.

'Ingrid.'

He'd stopped calling her Gran when he was fifteen. It seemed babyish as a teenager, and he wanted to annihilate all that back then. He regretted it when Sally died, wanted to have the family link again, so now he allowed himself to switch between the two.

She hugged him and stroked his head, and he felt pressure on his rib. He tensed his muscles, which made it worse. She noticed him flinching and pulled back. She went to take his hand and spotted the strapped fingers.

'For Christ's sake,' she said, 'what have you done to yourself?'

'I was in a plane crash, maybe you heard.'

'Oh, Thorfinn.'

He didn't like her using his full name, it felt too formal, but he said nothing.

Ingrid ran a finger along the splint. 'Are you OK?'

'I was lucky,' he said.

'Just awful. Folk have died, is that right?'

Finn nodded, head down.

She stroked his hair, her fingers at his temples, behind his ear. He leaned away as she found a cut at the back of his scalp.

'They're keeping me in tonight,' he said. 'Concussion. They don't want me having an aneurysm like Mum.'

'Don't talk like that.'

'I got off lightly. A fractured rib and a broken knuckle.'

'How did it happen?'

Finn looked at her. Cropped white hair pushed forward, blue-grey eyes full of mischief. Fair Isle jumper with a Nordic runes design, red jeans, smart boots. She was sixty-seven but looked closer to fifty, amazing considering she'd spent all her life battered by the elements up here. She'd worked the farm for thirty years, with her husband for the first twenty-five then on her own, before selling off the fields to a neighbour when she began to feel the aches and pains too much. The job at the Tomb of the Eagles seemed to have injected new life into her, though.

Finn thought about her question. 'I'm not sure. There was a lot of fog and turbulence, we were getting thrown around.'

She touched his cheek, which made tears come to his eyes. He breathed in and felt his ribs expand and contract. He was aware of his body struggling to hold itself together. He imagined the morphine seeping through his veins.

'You're probably still in shock,' Ingrid said.

She put her arms around him and he let himself be held like a baby. The release of it felt good, someone else taking control.

'I feel so guilty.'

Ingrid pulled back to make eye contact. 'It wasn't your fault.'

'You don't know what it was like.'

'I know that you're my grandson and a good boy, and whatever happens I'm here for you.'

He looked away.

She rubbed his arm. Finn remembered her doing the same thing as they sat in his living room in Dundee, the day after he found Sally. He was brutally hungover, had spent the rest of the previous day drinking and wandering from room to room, picking up things and putting them back down, lying down on her bed and smelling the pillow, staring at a photo of the two of them on holiday in Greece together, stupid smiles on their faces. But this was the next day, the truth starting to sink in. He was never going to see her again.

Ingrid had got the first ferry in the morning and driven down through the country. They held each other and cried until it seemed a ridiculous thing to keep doing, like they were imitating themselves being sad, falsifying their emotions. Cups of tea went cold on the low table in front of them as Finn flicked through some of his mum's drawings. She'd been skilful with a pencil, the reason she'd gone to art college in the first place. She'd never done enough with her degree. Having Finn so young she had to get on and make money, didn't have time to be unemployed. But she didn't blame Finn for that, and never accepted help from Ingrid. Finn couldn't understand either of those things. He blamed his own existence for Sally not becoming a proper artist, and he blamed her for not letting her own mother help her out in difficult circumstances. But Sally had always maintained she didn't have to work as an artist to be an artist, she was happy doodling away, sketching him as he played Mario Kart, or mucking about at the bandstand in Magdalen Green. He flicked the pages of her sketchbook, unable to take it in. Ingrid was next to him, the touch of her hand on his arm only highlighting the distance between them. How could Finn ever understand what it was like for Ingrid?

Losing her own daughter yet having to keep herself together for her grandson. He tried to think about that whenever he felt like wallowing in self-pity, but the grief swamped him all the same.

Now his stomach lurched as he remembered the plane last night, nosediving through the fog, the glance he shared with Oil Guy as they strapped themselves in, the look on Charlotte's face. He pictured the punch-up, flirting with Maddie, seeing her walk into the airport at the start.

His phone rang. It was in the pocket of his jeans but he couldn't get his hand in with the splint. He tried to reach round with his other hand but his rib growled in pain.

'Let me,' Ingrid said, pulling it out and handing it to him.

Amy.

'My God, Finn, are you all right?'

He remembered talking to her on the plane. Shit, had his phone done something to the electronics, was that why they crashed? No, that was crazy, he'd used it at the start of the flight, before everything else.

'Are you there?'

It seemed obscene that she was talking in Dundee and he could hear her. He imagined radio waves racing up through the fog and cloud, zinging above the earth, bouncing off the satellite and back down to the exact place he was now, trying to hold on.

'I'm fine,' he said.

'I was so worried. It's all over the news, your flight. Are you OK? Where are you?'

She had that flat Dundonian accent, same as him, the vowels smudged together like you didn't want to open your mouth too wide. The opposite of Orcadian with its rolling Rs, tone shifts and dancing rhythm.

'I'm in hospital,' he said. 'Ingrid's here. I'm OK. Broken rib and hand, that's all.'

'They said on the news seven people are dead?'

'Yeah.'

'How did it happen?'

Finn realised he would be asked that as long as he lived. He'd survived a fatal plane crash, it would define him for the rest of his life. He was inside a big story. Do you remember the plane that crashed in Orkney before Christmas that time? This guy is one of the survivors. Wow, what was it like, how did it happen, did you see anyone die, were you scared, I bet you were scared.

'I can't remember too well,' Finn said. 'I have concussion, they're keeping me in.'

'I'll come and see you.'

Finn shook his head. 'There's no point. I'll be out tomorrow, I'll come home then.'

He tried to imagine stepping on board a plane.

'I should be there,' Amy said.

'By the time you get here I could be back in Dundee. There probably won't be any flights for a while, I'll get the ferry. I'll be back before you know it.'

He tried to picture Amy in their flat. He supposed it was their home, the two of them, but it didn't feel like that. It was where he grew up, too many memories of Sally everywhere, her ghost haunting every room, every dinner plate, every air freshener, every stick of furniture. He wondered what it was like for Amy, stepping into the home of her boyfriend and his dead mother. How can you compete with that? But she never mentioned it, never complained or suggested they move. She never pushed him to get rid of any of Sally's stuff. He imagined her now, phone to her ear, pacing around the tight kitchen like she always did on a call, running her fingers along the worktop, absent-mindedly swiping crumbs to the floor.

He tried to remember how they got together in the first place. Their relationship seemed like a dream somehow, like he'd never fully been present in it. They met in the Art Bar, a basement dive just along from his flat, one of the first nights Finn went out after his mum's funeral, two months after. Some coursemates cajoled him into it. One of them was performing at an open mic. Amy was at the next table with a girl who was also doing a turn on the tiny stage. She seemed grown-up compared to his student mates, though she was the same age as him. It was easy, he didn't have to try too hard, just mentioned his dead mum and off they went together. Within three months she'd moved in and they were shopping for new cutlery and going for Sunday morning walks around Balgay Hill. It was almost too easy.

'If you're sure,' Amy said down the line.

'Trust me.'

There was a knock, then the door opened. It was the police officer from earlier, Linklater, with another cop, middle-aged, pot-bellied, saggy jowls like a bloodhound. Linklater gave Finn a look. Ingrid introduced herself with a firm handshake.

'I have to go,' Finn said. 'The police are here.'

10

The uniformed cop stood at the door and stared into space as Linklater walked to the bed.

Ingrid tried to give Finn a reassuring look.

'I'll be outside if you need me,' she said, closing the door.

Linklater looked at Finn's bandaged hand. 'What's the news from the doctor?'

'Six weeks to heal, same with the rib. They're keeping me in overnight.'

Surely she had already spoken to the doctor.

'You're lucky,' Linklater said.

'So everyone tells me,' Finn said, then regretted how it sounded.

The look on Linklater's face hardened. 'Seven people are dead.'

'I'm sorry.'

Linklater pulled her phone out and fiddled with it, then placed it on the bed.

'Do you mind if I record this conversation?'

'Is it an official interview?'

'Nothing formal, just a chat. I like to record everything, keeps everyone straight.'

'What if I refuse?'

'Then I won't record it. We'll speak at the station either way. This is just a chance to tell me what happened.'

Finn looked at the phone. A small red light blinked on the screen, along with a throbbing microphone icon. He remembered the light at the end of the wing, winking into the blackness, sending a signal into space.

'Well?' Linklater said.

'Sure.'

Linklater smiled. She looked like someone he might've got along with in different circumstances. She took a piece of paper out of her pocket and unfolded it. He could see the Loganair logo. 'We have a person unaccounted for. Madeleine Pierce. Someone you seem to know quite well.'

Finn shook his head. 'Not really.'

'You spent several hours talking to her at Kirkwall Airport. Had seven gin and tonics together, according to the woman who served you.'

'I never met her before that.'

'Really?'

'Yes.'

'So how did you get talking?'

'She came over to the bar to get away from those other guys on the plane. They were hassling her.'

Linklater looked at him. 'She was getting grief from strangers, so she started chatting and drinking with another stranger?'

'I suppose so.'

'You didn't think that was odd?'

'She said I didn't look threatening, something like that.'

Linklater raised her eyebrows. 'Did she say why she was travelling?'

Finn thought about that. 'No.'

'Nothing at all?'

Finn shook his head. 'Not that I can remember.'

'And you didn't ask?'

'No.'

'A two-hour delay, drinking at the airport and talking to someone, and you never asked why she was flying to Edinburgh?'

'I presume she would've told me if she'd wanted to.'

'What about you, what were you doing on Orkney?'

Finn nodded at the door. 'Visiting my gran. I came to catch up before Christmas. I was heading home.'

'Which is where?'

'Dundee. A flat on Perth Road.'

'So you were flying to Edinburgh then, what, bus or train?'

'Train.'

'Did you tell Mrs Pierce your plans?'

'She's married?'

Linklater smiled. 'She didn't mention it? Seems there's quite a lot our mysterious Madeleine didn't tell you.'

Linklater looked at the paper in her hand, peered at a handwritten scrawl in the margin. 'According to the electoral register she lives in Coplands Road in Stromness with her husband, Kevin.'

'Have you spoken to him?'

'An officer is heading there just now to talk to him. Tell me what you can remember about the flight.'

The room was too warm. Finn reached for a plastic cup of water next to his bed and took a sip. It tasted of chlorine and medicine. He coughed and put the cup down.

'I'm not sure,' he said.

Linklater gave him a look like he was a stroppy kid refusing to eat his broccoli. She pulled something out of her pocket. The severed plastic of his wrist and ankle restraints. She held them up.

'This needs explaining.'

'I went to the toilet. When I came back one of those other guys was in my seat, talking to Maddie.'

'One of the men who were hassling her at the airport?'

'Yes.'

'What sort of hassle are we talking about?'

'Trying to chat her up, but aggressive too. You know the kind of thing, they were drunk.'

'And you weren't?'

'That's different.'

'In what way?'

'It just is.'

'OK, so he was in your seat.'

'He was hurting Maddie, had a hold of her. She was scared.'

'So you assaulted him,' Linklater said, putting the restraints back in her pocket.

'It wasn't like that, I was trying to help her.'

'We have a statement from the stewardess saying that you hit him.'

'Is she OK?' Finn said.

'Who?'

Finn pictured her nametag. 'Charlotte.'

Linklater thought for a moment. 'She's physically fine but understandably traumatised.'

'What about the oil worker, the guy I fought with?'

'What makes you think he's an oil worker, did he say that?'

'The logo on his jacket,' Finn said. 'We weren't exactly on speaking terms.'

'Let your fists do the talking,' Linklater said.

'You've got it all wrong. I've never done anything like that before.'

'If you say so.'

'Is he OK?'

Linklater looked at the other officer then back. 'He's critical but stable. Lots of internal injuries. They've put him in an induced coma. We'll have to wait and see.'

'And his mates are all dead?' Finn said. 'Everyone else is dead?'

Linklater nodded. 'Except for Mrs Pierce, who's still missing.'

Finn rubbed his jaw, then his hand.

'What's his name?' Finn said.

'Who?'

'The guy I was fighting with.'

Linklater looked at the paper in her hand. 'Sean Bayliss.'

Finn rolled the name around under his breath like a prayer.

'Tell me about the fight,' Linklater said.

'One minute we were arguing, the next we were on the floor and people were pulling us off each other.'

Finn wanted to grab the paper out of Linklater's hand. He wanted to see the names of the dead, read their obituaries, find out about their lives, who they loved, who loved them in return, whether their lives had worked out like they hoped.

He felt something in his guts and his tongue began to sweat.

'Pass me that,' he said through his teeth, pointing at a basin on the floor by the bed. Linklater handed it to him and stepped back as he vomited into it, just bile, nothing in his stomach. It burned at the lining of his throat. He spat, took a sip of water and spat again.

'Do you need a nurse?' Linklater said.

He waved that away and put the bowl next to the bed. The smell was rancid.

'So the stewardess put the restraints on you,' Linklater said.

'Yeah.'

'And the co-pilot did the same to Mr Bayliss.'

'Yes.'

'Then what?'

'If you've spoken to Charlotte, you know what happened.'

'I just want to get things clear.'

'The pilot announced we were heading back to Kirkwall, because of the disturbance.'

'Then?'

'Maddie didn't want to. She went to see him.'

'She went in the cockpit?'

Finn nodded.

'What did she do?'

'I don't know, the door was closed. But she came out. The co-pilot and the stewardess were trying to get in when she opened the door and came out. Then the plane was all over the place, we must've hit more turbulence. I felt my stomach going.'

'She definitely left the cockpit?'

'Yeah. The cabin was lurching, everyone tried to get to a seat and strap in. It was obvious something was wrong.'

'Did you see the pilot at this point?'

'No, I was getting my seatbelt on.'

'Then the plane hit the ground?'

Finn looked out the window and nodded. 'It broke in two straight away. A propeller and a wing came through the cabin.'

'Could you see Mrs Pierce at this point?'

'No. She was at the front of the plane, in the other half.'

'So you didn't see her at all during the crash.'

'No.'

'And you didn't see her after the plane stopped?'

Finn looked at Linklater. 'I didn't see her.'

'Are you sure?'

'Definite.'

Linklater thought about what he'd said for a while, a frown on her face.

'She had a bag,' she said eventually.

'What?'

'A brown leather holdall.'

Finn got an image of Maddie reaching over and pulling the bag from under the seat. 'I think so.'

Linklater looked sceptical. 'You were with her for hours, you didn't notice?'

'She did,' Finn said. 'I remember now.'

'What did she do with it on the plane?'

'Put it under the seat in front.'

'At the back of the plane?'

'Yes.'

'It's not there.'

'Sorry?'

'The bag.'

Linklater walked to the end of the bed.

Finn glanced down at the phone blinking away, recording every word. 'Maybe it got thrown out the cabin in the crash.'

Linklater nodded. 'Maybe.'

Finn was exhausted. The morphine, the sickness, the pain swarming his body. Adrenaline had kept him going through the shock, but now his body was giving up and his eyes drooped.

Linklater looked at him. 'That's probably enough for now.' She came round the side of the bed and picked up her phone. 'I'll need to speak to you again tomorrow.'

'I was hoping I could go back to Dundee.'

Linklater laughed. 'Wow.'

'What?'

She shook her head. 'At the very least you'll be charged with assault and endangering the lives of other passengers. Then there's the possibility of terrorist charges. And manslaughter.'

Finn's eyes widened. 'But all I did was fight with a guy.'

'Seven people are dead.'

'I didn't kill them.'

'But your actions might well have brought about their deaths.'

'I just want to go home.'

'Don't even think about leaving Orkney. I'm not arresting you, but until we get this sorted you'll have to stay on the islands.'

Finn raised his hand to his face and it shook, the edge of the metal splint scratching at his cheek.

Linklater nodded to the other officer, who opened the door. She turned to Finn.

'You have no idea how much trouble you're in.'

11

He slept like shit despite the morphine. Every time he shifted his weight his body complained. His chest ached and his hand throbbed. He pressed the buzzer some time in the night and an older nurse with grey streaks in her hair handed him some pills. It was clear from her expression that she thought he should suck it up. He couldn't blame her, he would've been the same in her position. He wished he could just get over it, walk out of here, fly south and never have to think about any of it again.

He dreamt about Maddie, having sex with her in the aeroplane toilet. He was disgusted with himself, the workings of his subconscious, his hard-on when he woke.

He swung one leg then the other off the bed and eased his feet on to the cold floor. He held his shoulder blades and cricked his neck with a crunch. Wound his arms in slow circles like an old man doing t'ai chi. Felt the grind of the bones in the joints, loose after the crash, muscles stretching and aching under his left nipple.

A knock on the door.

Finn looked at the clock. Half eight. So it was starting already.

'Come in.'

A large woman swept into the room, smart suit and neat hair. Her broad smile and kind eyes suggested that she'd seen plenty of life, not all of it straightforward.

'Hello there,' she said in a local accent. 'My name is Janet Jott, and you must be Thorfinn Sullivan.'

'Finn,' he said.

'Finn, exactly so.'

'Who are you?'

'Of course.' She strode towards him, holding his gaze. 'I work with the police and local authorities. I'm a counsellor. A trauma counsellor, not a politician.'

'Is that so.'

'I mostly work as a marriage counsellor, but I'm trained in trauma as well.'

'Why are you here?'

'To assess you.' She lifted a hand and waved something at him. 'Here's my card.'

Finn took it and laid it on the bed without looking at it. 'I'm fine.'

'I'm sure you are, I just need to have a wee chat.'

'There's no need.'

'There is if you want to get out of hospital today.'

There was an edge to her, behind the round body and grin.

'Fine,' Finn said.

She asked him how he felt and he said fine. She asked how he'd slept and he said fine. She asked if he was having any flashbacks to the events of last night and he said no. She asked a dozen more questions about him and his life, his mind and body, his reaction to the crash, whether he felt sad or happy or in pain or confused or weak or guilty. He said he was fine, fine, fine. Anything to get this over with and get out the door.

'I actually know your grandmother,' Janet said. 'She asked me to come.'

‘Really?’

‘Someone would’ve come anyway but she wanted me to do it, as a friend.’

Finn thought about that. Ingrid didn’t suffer fools gladly and she didn’t make friends easily.

‘Is Ingrid here?’ Finn said.

Janet nodded. ‘She stayed last night. Slept down the hall in the nurses’ area. She’s worried sick, as you can imagine.’

Finn rubbed at the stubble on his chin.

‘Anyway,’ Janet said, ‘you don’t seem to be suffering any major psychological trauma at the moment.’

‘At the moment?’

Janet folded her arms. ‘People often get post-traumatic stress, which doesn’t necessarily manifest in the first hours, days or even weeks. It can strike at any time.’

‘I’m OK.’

‘But you’ve experienced a highly extreme situation. And you are showing some signs of anger and aggression.’

‘Can I leave hospital or not?’

Janet touched her cheek as if contemplating the options. ‘I think so. But I want to make an appointment to meet you again, as a follow-up. Shall we say tomorrow at twelve? I’ll get Ingrid to remind you. My office address is on the card, as is my phone number if you want to talk before then.’

Finn picked up the card and flicked it between his fingers.

Janet continued. ‘The police will be in touch, of course.’

‘I spoke to Linklater already.’

Janet nodded. ‘She’s very sharp. A dog with a bone, that one.’

She pulled a pen and a couple of forms out of her handbag and Finn struggled to sign them with his splinted hand.

'After the doctor gives you the once-over on her morning rounds you're free to go. But remember, if things get on top of you at any point, please call me.'

12

They slipped out of the ward through the staff entrance then doubled back and cut through Orthopaedics to get to Ingrid's car, parked outside ENT. Janet had told them that a young woman from the *Orcadian* was outside the front of the building so Finn ducked down as they left.

He sat up as they hit the road south out of Kirkwall.

'Was she there?'

Ingrid nodded.

'Just her?'

'Yes.'

Only one local journalist, he was lucky so far. Radio Orkney would be on the case. The big guns from the BBC and STV hadn't made it up yet because of the airport closure, same with the tabloids. But they'd be here soon, so he didn't have long.

Ingrid's old Skoda chugged up the hill on the outskirts of town. They passed the Highland Park distillery, its warehouses and pagoda roofs black with the fungus that lives on alcohol fumes. Finn opened his window to fill his nostrils with the reek of it.

'Can we take the Deerness road?' he said.

Ingrid glanced at him. 'I don't think that's a good idea.'

'Please.'

The Deerness road was where the airport was. It was out of their way, but not by much. There were four roads out of

Kirkwall, spread like a haphazard spider's web on the map. The high road west went past the tourist sites of Maes Howe, Stenness and Brodgar, the low road skirted the coast through Orphir with views over to Hoy. They were on the south road, heading back to Ingrid's cottage on South Ronaldsay. The Deerness road slunk southeast past the airport and Deer Sound, out to the remote beaches around the Gloup.

'I don't see what good it will do,' Ingrid said.

'I need to see,' Finn said.

Ingrid put her indicator on, turned left past a farm and bumped along a rough track until she hit the A road and went right. They headed downhill to the flat plain where the airfield sat. The road cut past landing lights, small yellow pylons standing in two lines, a robot army waiting for the order to attack.

The sky was bright, broken clouds flitting east over Inganess Bay. Finn tried to remember this place from last night, the darkness, the fog, the cold, the scream of the engines.

The Skoda was buffeted by a westerly and shuddered as Ingrid moved down through the gears for a bend. They came over a rise and saw the airfield. The low-slung concrete cube of the arrivals and departures building, the stumpy control tower, barely poking its head above the surrounding fields, the rusted grey hangar to the side.

There were emergency vehicles all over the runway, people hanging around in hi-vis jackets. Finn pictured the propellers cutting through the cabin, tons of metal spinning hundreds of times a second, slicing through the air. The sheer dumb power of it, even in a tiny plane, made him feel weak.

Their car slowed. A burly old cop with grey hair was waving them down at the entrance to the airport. Finn glanced at the car park, just a handful of hire cars and two police vehicles.

Ingrid pulled over and wound the window down.

'Ross,' she said.

'It's yourself, Ingrid,' the officer said. He rested his hand on the roof of the car and leaned over. 'And the lad.'

'It is.'

Finn caught the look the cop gave him. Blame. He'd have to get used to that. He stared at his broken hand, rubbed the splint. Felt his chest rise and fall, his ribs stretch and contract, the pain slide along them.

'Terrible business,' Ross said.

Ingrid had her hands on the wheel. 'Aye.'

'Terrible business,' Ross said again to himself.

Ingrid nodded beyond the terminal building to the tarmac. 'How's it going?'

'All right.'

'What are you up to?'

'We're after the missing lassie. Stopping folk, in case they've seen anything.'

'She's still not turned up?'

Ross shook his head. 'They thought maybe she was thrown clear, but we haven't found anything.'

He meant a body.

'Well, if she was out all night, she'll have hypothermia by now,' Ingrid said.

The cop looked at Finn. 'We just don't know, do we? We don't know.'

Finn was surprised to hear his own voice bounce around inside the car. 'I hope you find her.'

Ross paused. 'Me too. There's enough dead folk already.'

The cop thought Finn was the reason, the killer. The lad responsible for the biggest death toll on Orkney since the Vikings.

Ross looked behind the Skoda. Finn glanced in the side mirror and saw another car coming up. The cop straightened and gave two taps on their car roof. 'Better get this next one, Ingrid.'

'No problem.'

'Let me know if you hear any news. And obviously if his nibs here remembers anything.'

'Of course.'

Talking about him as if he wasn't there, treating him like a little kid. It was no more than he deserved. Finn's face flushed.

Ingrid wound the window up and drove on.

Finn craned his neck to keep the runway in sight. In between fire engines he caught glimpses of the wreckage, the crumpled face of the cockpit, the ragged edge where the fuselage was torn apart, the broken wing.

He thought about Maddie. Had she found shelter or was she lying in a ditch, frozen to death?

They passed the turn for Tankerness then over the hill and the airport was gone. Finn closed his eyes and pictured Maddie playing with her gin and tonic at the bar, eyes flicking up, licking lime juice from her finger.

He took a breath that stung his left lung, then coughed, pain slicing through his chest. He lifted his hand away from his mouth and there was a light spray of pink blood across the palm. He got a tissue and wiped it away, checking to make sure Ingrid hadn't noticed.

'Did you see the counsellor?' she said, eyes on the road.

'Yeah.'

'Janet's a good woman, knows her job. She's not had her troubles to seek.'

They trundled in silence past Groatsetter and Veltigar, bleak brown fields on either side, sheep grazing where they could. Ingrid turned right at the Bay of Suckquoy, towards St Mary's.

Finn felt Ingrid's hand on his leg. A couple of reassuring squeezes, then she lifted it to change gear. She glanced at him.

'Let's just get you home. Everything will be fine.'

13

They pulled up outside Ingrid's cottage. As the engine cut, the whoop of the wind took over and the car rocked. Finn eased himself out, holding on to the door in case it caught in a gust. Ingrid looked at him over the roof of the car. He smiled and turned to gaze over the firth. He was always amazed by the view from here. High on this southern headland, they could see for miles over the Pentland Firth to Muckle Skerry, its lighthouse a thin needle against the horizon, then west to Stroma and the Scottish mainland, a muscled shoulder of land peeking through successive squalls of rain blowing across the country towards Scandinavia.

'Come on in,' Ingrid said. 'I'll get the kettle on.'

Finn shook his head. 'I need some air, I think I'll walk along to see the old guys.'

Ingrid frowned at him, her hair whipping in the wind. 'You need rest.'

Finn rubbed at his scalp. 'I need to clear my head.' He walked round and touched her arm. 'It's fine.' He kissed her cheek and zipped his coat up as he headed back along the road.

'Don't get blown off a cliff,' Ingrid said.

He raised his good hand and walked away. 'The old guys' was a joke between the two of them, how they referred to the Neolithic skeletons along the road in the Tomb of the Eagles. About half a mile, hang a right at the visitor centre then north along the headland and you got to the ancient site, a burial cairn from five thousand years ago, full of dead bodies and the eagle bones that gave the place its name. It was found by old Eddie Lewis on his farm years ago after a storm, the wind ripping away topsoil to expose the structure. The Lewises still ran the place as a tourist attraction, one of the few on the island not tied up by Historic Scotland. Lewis deserved credit for looking after it. Everyone on the islands knew stories of farmers who'd found similar remains on their land but had kicked the mud back in place to avoid the disruption a historical find would bring. Orkney felt like it must've been seething with life back then, at a time when the Egyptians were building pyramids and the Greeks were marching into Persia. And here, on this little rock halfway to the Arctic, communities were living and thriving without drawing attention to themselves. Finn loved that.

The Tomb of the Eagles was closed to the public over the winter, except by appointment. The Lewises used tourist money to take themselves off to a timeshare in Lanzarote for three months, leaving Ingrid to arrange the occasional tour. Orkney wasn't a winter destination and tourists rarely made it to the furthest tip of the islands, preferring to canter around the more accessible Ring of Brodgar, Maes Howe and Skara Brae.

So Finn and Ingrid had the place to themselves for the most part. Sometimes, when the weather closed in and the waves battered the shore beneath Ingrid's cottage, it felt like they were the only people on earth. Other times, when the clouds lifted, the expanse of sea and sky was breathtaking. A couple of farmhouses further back from the coast were the only other signs of civilisation for miles, their sheep shuffling to the fence at feeding time. Finn loved the isolation, the solitude.

He was almost there now, smears of leftover snow in the dark crannies of the field. The way the headland looped round, the sea was on his right now, nothing for hundreds of miles until Norway. Finn imagined Vikings ploughing through icy waves, preparing to land.

He reached the tomb. Nothing much to look at from this side, just a grassy hillock until you turned the corner and saw the stone wall and small square opening. He pulled the rope out of the hole, bringing the low trolley with it. This was part of the appeal for tourists, the ramshackle spirit of the experience. They had to lie on the thing and pull the rope to get in. Finn looked out to sea at the shimmering waves then lay down, his rib aching, and pulled until he was inside and the silence shrouded him.

It was larger than looked possible from the outside, a Stone Age Tardis. The roof was three metres high, light streaming in through plastic-covered holes. The dirt was packed down, millennia of visitors trampling the space, countless steps in and out. He'd been coming here for as long as he could remember, a space to think.

To his left was a row of five skulls. They'd been found in a heap with others, which were now down at the visitor centre along with the eagle bones. But the Lewises had decided to leave some here in situ for the tourists, like a deathly chorus line. Finn liked to imagine them commenting sarcastically on tourists after they left, bitching and gossiping. Right now he felt they were mocking him, toothy grins laughing at his situation. He'd cheated death, but what about the others on the plane with families and friends grieving for them?

He sat on the ground and closed his eyes, listened to the wind. The muffled sound of it made him feel like he was in a cocoon.

The plink of his ringtone made him flinch. He was surprised to get a signal out here. He slid his phone out with his good hand and looked at the screen. Not someone in his address book and not a number he recognised.

'Hello?'

Silence for a few seconds, then a voice he knew.

'Hi, Finn.'

'Jesus, Maddie, where are you?'

'I didn't know who else to turn to.'

'The police are looking for you.'

'I know.'

'You left us,' Finn said.

'I had my reasons.'

'Fuck's sake, I could've been dying.'

'You were OK, I checked,' she said. 'Don't you remember?'

Finn frowned. 'I'm not sure what I remember. What about the others? Did you check on them?'

Nothing down the line.

Eventually Finn spoke. 'Were you outside all night?'

'No.'

'Where are you?'

There was a long pause.

'I'm in a cowshed.' She laughed under her breath. 'It stinks but it's warm.'

'Are you hurt?'

'I'm fine,' Maddie said. 'I mean, I've been better but I'm OK.'

Finn looked at the skulls staring at him. 'You need to go home.'

'That's the last place I'm going.'

'Why didn't you tell me you were married?'

'I'm not.'

'So the police have it wrong?'

'I'm leaving him,' Maddie said. 'I mean I've left him.'

'The police have sent someone to your house, see if you went back there.'

'Christ, that's all I need.'

Finn walked up and down, dragging his fingertips along the wall. 'Look, whatever's going on, the police can sort it out.'

'I can't go to the police.'

'Why not?'

'They'll make me go back.'

'They won't.'

'You have no idea,' Maddie said. 'He manipulates people, twists them round his finger. He'll persuade them we're a happy couple, and I won't get another chance to get away.'

'That's ridiculous.'

'You don't know.' Anger in her voice overtaking the fear.

'Take it easy.'

'He'll paint me as some psychotic bitch and the police will believe him, especially after all this shit with the plane.'

Finn took a breath and heard her do the same. The wind whistled outside the cairn. Finn looked up at the hole in the roof and saw clouds racing east. He put his hand to his rib.

'I need your help,' Maddie said.

'Why me?'

'I don't have anyone else. All my friends are his friends. I'm alone.'

'What do you want?'

'I want to get off these stupid islands. I can't believe what happened on the plane, this is so fucked up.'

'You just left,' Finn said.

'What?'

'You left us there, Maddie, in the plane.'

'I told you, I couldn't go back.'

'But people were injured. You could've helped.'

'The ambulances were already on the runway.'

'People died.'

'I know.'

'Seven people.'

Silence for a beat.

'Christ,' she said.

Finn walked the length of the chamber. The skulls smiled at him.

'Give me one reason why I should help you,' he said. 'Why I shouldn't just hang up.'

'I need you,' Maddie said. 'I've got no one else.'

'Go to the police.'

'I've told you, I can't.'

'I don't believe you.'

'If you don't help me, I'll die.'

The last word caught in her throat. Finn closed his eyes, saw two empty glasses on the bar at the airport, the shape of her legs in those jeans. He pictured the cabin jerking and twisting, ripping apart, the propeller slicing through metal like it was nothing.

'What do you want me to do?'

'I need somewhere to lie low,' Maddie said. 'Until I work things out. I can't stay in this shed, the farmer's already been in this morning for milking, I almost got caught. Can you think of somewhere I could hide until I get my shit together?'

14

He was almost at St Margaret's Hope when he saw the familiar sign for the cemetery at St Peter's Kirk off to the right. Sod it, Maddie could wait in the cowshed another half hour. He turned at the war memorial, went past the houses of Haybrake and Brandyquoy. He smiled at the place names, Orkney was full of quirky ones. Already on the few miles from Ingrid's place he'd passed Suckquoy, Mucklehouse, Wasbister and Quoyhorsetter. Every stretch of road was like a little found poem in your mouth.

It was only a couple of miles over a rise in the land, sheep and cows grazing in grassy fields. The road was single-track with passing places as he went over a crossroads and past a lone, nameless standing stone surrounded by greylag geese. The North Sea was dead ahead as the road sloped down to the shore and ended at the kirk, a simple eighteenth-century block of grey stone with green moss spread across the slate roof.

A track stretched from the church down to the beach and headland beyond. Marram grass was threatening to engulf the track, which disappeared before it reached the sand.

Finn got out and closed the car door. He opened the low iron gate to the graveyard and went in. He felt tiny grains of rusted metal on his fingers. This was a new part of the cemetery, not like the ancient graveyards scattered all over the islands, and yet the elements had already set about the gate, the stone dyke and the gravestones.

The area where Sally was buried was still half empty. Finn wondered where they would put people once it filled up. Burying people was unsustainable, wasn't it? If you maintained and respected each grave forever, the whole planet would eventually be full of rotting corpses. And yet there was no crematorium in Orkney, so that hadn't been an option.

He and Ingrid had discussed the funeral, but he couldn't remember much about it. At some point she'd asked about burial or cremation, Dundee or Orkney. Dundee was Finn's home but despite twenty years living there it didn't feel like Sally's. Finn was fine with her being brought north and laid to rest next to her dad.

He walked to the grave. He'd visited twice in the last week, the polished black granite so familiar to him. He looked at the headstone and tried to conjure something up in his mind. An image of Sally smiling at him over a shared double pepperoni in Pizza Express, the look on her face when he told her he'd been accepted into Duncan of Jordanstone. He remembered her crying at the end of a documentary about whales. It wasn't even sad, she was just overwhelmed by their grace in the water. Then she laughed, called herself ridiculous as she wiped the tears away and got up to put the kettle on. He'd been embarrassed at the time, a teenager trying to distance himself from the generation that spawned him. What a waste of time it was trying to be different, trying to be original, when we're all just the same.

He looked beyond the kirk. He could see the next headland south of here, then the one behind that, jutting out into the water like they thought they would last forever. But they would crumble into the sea eventually, just like this churchyard and all the bodies underground. Beyond that second headland, a few miles round the coast, was the Tomb of the Eagles and Ingrid's place. You could walk it on a good day with the right boots.

He looked back at the grave and his grandad's stone beside it. Ingrid would be next, he supposed, there was a space for her on the other side. What about him, what would happen to him when he died? Who would take care of that?

He ran a finger along the top of Sally's gravestone.

'I don't think I understood how much I would miss you.'

He straightened up and looked around. No human activity anywhere, just grass and sand, sea and sky.

'I'm involved in something, Mum,' he said. 'And I don't know how to get out of it.'

He breathed in and felt his eyes grow wet. He swallowed and turned his head away from the wind off the sea. He thought about the seven dead people waiting to be put into the ground. He thought about the survivors, Sean in a coma, Charlotte in shock. And Maddie hiding in a byre.

He turned away from the grave and walked back to the car. He didn't look back.

15

The wind rocked the car as he crossed the Churchill Barrier on to Glimps Holm. Just a few hundred yards then he was on the next barrier, a thin causeway exposed to the full brunt of the weather off Scapa Flow. The sunken blockships in the sea to his right always filled him with a strange melancholy, like lives of neighbours half glimpsed in the corner of your eye. Their original purpose, to stop U-boats entering Scapa Flow during the war, was long behind them now, and their skeletal remains were an unsettling graveyard, an array of rusted and decayed hulls and decks protruding from the wash. He thought of the remains of the Loganair plane sitting on the runway. How would they get rid of all that wreckage? What happens to planes after the investigators have finished with them?

On Lamb Holm he drove past the Italian Chapel, another sobering sight. During the war the Nissen hut had been turned into a beautiful church by Italian prisoners of war in their spare time. Finn thought about those prisoners here at the top of the world, far from home, stuck in the country they were at war with. A car was parked by the side of the last barrier and Finn spotted two wetsuited figures a hundred yards out in the bay. He dreaded to think what the water temperature was like this time of year, something to stop the heart.

On the walk back from the tomb to the cottage Finn had been working out an excuse for borrowing Ingrid's car, but when he came into the living room she was napping on the sofa, a cold cup of tea on the table by her side. He'd lifted the key and crept out.

Now at Bendigo, on the outskirts of Kirkwall, a car was stationary in front of him. There was a police car pulled over on the verge and an officer in a yellow jacket was leaning in the window talking to the driver. Not a roadblock but the same low-key thing they had at the airport. They would have them on all roads leading from the area, checking if anyone had seen Maddie. Finn had been expecting it.

It was a young woman officer, dark hair in a side plait, glasses, small frame. Finn wound his window down. He didn't recognise her but she raised her eyebrows when she saw him.

'You're out of hospital, then,' she said.

So he was notorious already. Everyone in Orkney knew him, knew what he'd been involved in.

She patted the side of the car.

'Where you headed?'

'Tesco, getting the messages for my gran,' Finn said.

'You think that's a good idea?'

'Why not?'

'Showing yourself in public, so soon after.'

Finn hadn't planned on it at all but now realised he'd have to go there to back up his story.

'I can't hide forever,' he said.

The officer turned as a car pulled up behind Finn. 'I take it you haven't seen anything of this Madeleine woman?'

Finn shook his head. 'I told Linklater everything I know.'

'Fair enough. See you in a bit.'

'Sorry?'

The officer peered into the car. 'When you come back with the shopping.'

'Of course.' Finn wound the window up, put the car in gear and drove away.

He headed into town, pulled up in Tesco's car park and went inside. It was busy. It felt like everyone's eyes were on him as he wandered round with his basket. He was sure they were talking about him as he walked up and down the aisles. He would have to buy a decent amount of stuff, make the journey worthwhile, but he had no idea what Ingrid needed, so he just began picking things up. Milk, bread, fruit, crisps, juice, the Tunnock's teacakes she liked. When he had enough he went to the checkout, felt like a sitting duck, an easy target. Blood rushed to his cheeks as he paid and took the bags outside.

He put the shopping in the passenger seat then drove east, making to head out on the airport road then turning left on to Inganess Road, which soon became single-track with passing places outside town. He slowed at each building, unsure which one Maddie was in. He went past three farms with outhouses and sheds clustered together, but kept on driving.

The road sloped down to Inganess Bay then ended in a tiny car park opposite the beach. One car was parked and Finn saw an old man walking a retriever along the shoreline. The guy was wrapped in a scarf, hat and gloves, two jackets as well, the wind rippling the dog's fur. Out in the bay was another rusted old ship, prow poking towards land as if it had died in a final attempt to reach shore. These were dangerous waters. The skeletons of hundreds of ships lay around the coastline.

In the other direction was the airport. He was round the back of it now, could see it spread towards the high road he'd taken earlier with Ingrid. This was the sea he could hear and smell last night, the bay next to the airfield. This was the way Maddie came as she strode from the wreckage. There was no security anywhere. Finn got out the car and walked to the edge of the airfield. The wind blasted his face as he pulled a woolly hat down over his ears and thrust his hands into his jacket pockets. A four-foot fence was all that separated the airport from the surrounding land, bedraggled wires strung between posts that hugged the coast along a rocky outcrop. He approached a gate, mud squelching under his trainers on the rough track. Three signs were tied to the gate with cable ties similar to the restraints he'd had round his wrists and ankles.

Emergency Exit, Keep Clear, written in black on yellow.

No Public Access Beyond This Point, a red circle with a diagonal line through it, some guy shoving his hand out to say no, in case you didn't get the point.

And last a flimsy blue cardboard sign that read *Kirkwall Airport Bylaws Apply Beyond This Point*. Finn wondered what those bylaws were. Don't get involved in a plane crash? Don't cause seven deaths? Don't leave a crime scene? Don't help someone you hardly know evade the police?

He put his hands on the metal of the gate just to feel the cold of it against his skin, then went back to the car, nodding at the dog walker on the beach. He turned the car and headed back up the hill, this time at a crawl, peering out the windscreen at each farm building. From this direction he noticed the red corrugated-iron door that Maddie had described. He nudged the car into the nearest passing place, switched the engine off and sat thinking. He couldn't just drive up to a cowshed. What if the farmer was inside? But he needed to get Maddie into the car without being seen.

He got out and walked towards the barn as if he knew what he was doing. He went straight into the building without looking round, thinking that would seem suspicious. The place smelled ripe and sour, dung and animal. Cows shuffled in their enclosures, their breath billowing from their noses. He got his phone out and called her number. Three rings then he hung up, like they agreed.

She stepped out from a stall at the end of the shed. She was silhouetted against the light from the other entrance as she came towards him. He felt excited and sick, a little dizzy. She had the same sway to her walk, her bag slung over her shoulder.

'You came.'

'I said I would.'

She grabbed him and held on in a hug. The smell of her hair came to him through the musty air of livestock and hay. He put a hand on the back of her head as he felt her breathing quicken and shoulders shake.

'It's OK,' he said.

She lifted her head. 'I'm sorry.'

'Don't be.'

Finn looked around. They were exposed here, large doorways at either end.

'We should go.'

He led her along the length of the shed then signalled for her to stop at the entrance. He went out a few feet and looked around. The Skoda was thirty yards down the road. Beyond that another car was starting up the hill from the car park. The dog walker. Finn ducked inside the barn till it was past, then took Maddie by the hand and walked to the car. He unlocked it and opened the boot.

'Get in.'

Maddie looked at him.

Finn nodded at the horizon. 'There are roadblocks. I went through one on the way here.'

'Christ.'

Maddie threw her bag in and squeezed into the tight space.

Finn stood holding the boot.

'Can I trust you?' she said.

'You have to.'

He closed the boot and got in the driver's seat. He wasn't used to being in charge. He swung the car out of the passing place, hyper-aware of the vehicle's motion, how it must feel in the boot. He nipped through town then south, back the way he'd come. The same cop on the road flagged him and he slowed, then stopped and wound his window down.

'Got your gran's messages,' she said, nodding at the plastic bags in the passenger seat.

'Yeah.'

'Took you a while.'

Finn shrugged.

There would be witnesses if she asked, plenty of people had seen him walking up and down the aisles.

'On you go,' the officer said. 'And take it easy on the barriers, the wind's up, they might be getting closed today.'

The engine crunched as Finn fumbled with the gearstick then got going, heading over the hill towards South Ronaldsay, wiping the sweat from his palms on to his jeans.

16

He drove the Skoda into the visitor centre car park and pulled up next to the entrance. The car park was empty except for the Tomb of the Eagles van, large brown logo on its side. The Lewises used in the summer, but it just sat here when they were away. He got out and opened the boot. Maddie blinked and squinted in the light, held a hand up to shield her eyes.

'Are you OK?' he said.

She held her hand out. 'Lucky I'm not claustrophobic.'

Finn looked around as he helped her out of the boot. The visitor centre was halfway between the tomb and Ingrid's cottage, but there was enough of a slope before the headland that Ingrid wouldn't be able to see them here.

'Come on,' he said. He led her to the doorway and fumbled some keys out of his pocket. Opened the mortice and Yale, punched the alarm into the box and went in.

'The Tomb of the Eagles?' Maddie said.

'You know it?'

'I was here years ago with Kev.'

Her face clouded over as Finn shut the door behind them. His phone rang. Ingrid. He declined the call.

'You'll be safe here,' he said, leading Maddie into the main room. The visitor centre was three rooms of exhibits built on to the side of the Lewises' home. With them away and no tours booked it was the safest place Finn could think of. His first idea of Maddie staying in the actual tomb was crazy. She needed sleep, warmth, food, a working toilet.

Finn's phone buzzed in his pocket, Ingrid again.

Maddie ran a hand along a thigh bone sitting on a display bench. 'How do you have keys to this place?'

'My gran looks after it while the owners are away.'

'And the owners are away?'

Finn nodded. 'For the next couple of months. They spend the winters somewhere hot.'

'But the tomb is still open?'

'Appointment only. We hardly ever get tour groups this time of year. If we get any I'll know in advance. I'll check with Ingrid.'

'Ingrid?'

'My gran.' Finn felt his pocket buzz again. 'I should get back, she's worried. But we need to talk first.'

Maddie stopped looking at the exhibits and turned to him. She caught the serious expression on his face. 'What about?'

Finn angled his head. 'You know what about, tell me what the hell is going on.'

'What do you mean?'

'Come on, I'll put the kettle on.'

He went through to the small kitchenette next to the public toilet, filled a kettle at the sink and switched it on.

He turned and Maddie was behind him in the doorway.

'If I'm going to help you, you need to tell me everything,' he said. 'We need to be completely honest.'

She was beautiful. With daylight streaming through the window, Finn could make out her features better than yesterday at the airport or earlier today in the byre. Deeper crows' feet around her eyes, the weary way she set her mouth, a vulnerability to her body language as she wavered at the door. It was a world away from the confident woman she appeared to be last night. Finn liked this Maddie more, she seemed real.

'Ask me anything and I'll tell you the truth,' she said.

Finn finished making coffee in mugs and handed her one.

'Let's sit through there,' he said, nodding at the next room. There were two stools at a display about excarnation. The people who lived here used to leave their dead out on the cliff top so that the remains were picked clean by sea eagles and other birds. A method of returning themselves to the world. Eagle food was not a bad way to go, Finn thought.

'Tell me why you were on the plane last night,' he said.

Maddie looked out the window and took a breath.

'I was leaving Orkney for ever.'

'Why?'

She turned a look on him. 'Because I'd just walked in on my husband screwing my best friend. The oldest bullshit in the world. Men have been fucking their wives' best friends ever since these guys were alive.' She waved a hand at the bones. 'I'm such an idiot.'

'What did he say when you found him?'

Maddie shook her head. 'I didn't give him the chance to say anything. What could he say, that he was sorry, it wasn't what it looked like? He was pounding away on her, the pair of them screaming the house down.'

'Why not just move out?' Finn said. 'Why jump straight on a plane?'

'You don't know Kev, he's a bully. This has been coming for ages. I was glad of the chance to get away while he still had his pants down. He's such a shit, he twists things around, has to be in control. If I hadn't got on that plane he would've found me and dragged me back. I would've been imprisoned.'

'You don't seem like the kind of woman who lets herself be controlled like that.'

Maddie sighed and looked around the room. 'You don't know me.'

'When the plane turned round you acted like it was a death sentence,' Finn said. 'Surely it's not that bad, surely you could've laid low somewhere until he forgot about you?'

'It's not as simple as that. I made sure I could never go back.'

'How?'

Maddie lifted her bag off the floor and unzipped it. She pushed aside some make-up and a purse, clothes and underwear, and lifted out a carrier bag. She held it open. Twenty-pound notes. Thousands in neat bundles with elastic bands.

'Shit,' Finn said. 'How much?'

'Hundred thousand.'

'It's his?'

Maddie nodded. 'Kev is up to his neck in illegal crap.'

'How does he make it?'

'Does salvage runs in Scapa Flow with his mate Lenny. They strip the sunken fleet and flog it. They also pick up dubious deliveries from overseas in his boat.'

'Isn't taking this asking for trouble?'

'It's my divorce settlement, ten years of loyal service.'

Finn took a sip of his coffee as Maddie put the money away. Silence for a moment. Out the window were just brown fields and sheep. The smell of the sea filtered into the room.

'I want to talk about the crash,' Finn said eventually.

A look passed between them that made Finn think she understood him. She was the only one who could understand because she'd been through the same thing.

'What happened in the cockpit?' he said. 'You were alone with the pilot for a few minutes.'

'I didn't do anything.'

'You must've done something.'

'Are you saying the crash was my fault?'

'I'm not saying that.'

'If anything it was your fault.' Maddie put her mug down. 'If you hadn't got in a stupid fight none of this would've happened.'

'That's not fair.'

'It's just as fair as saying I did something to the pilot.'

'Take it easy.'

'I asked him to turn round, head for Edinburgh. He said no. He radioed the tower and told them to send police, then he asked me to leave.'

'And you just left?'

'What else could I do, fly the plane? I realised I was being an idiot. I came out, but that's when we hit turbulence.'

Finn looked down at his coffee. 'I've replayed it a thousand times in my head. I can't help it.'

'Me too.'

'Seven people are dead. Just you, me, Charlotte and Sean left.'

'Who's Sean?'

'The guy who hassled you. He's in a coma.'

'How's the stewardess?'

'Suffering from shock.'

'You think we're in shock?'

'It doesn't matter what you call it.'

'I suppose not.' Maddie lifted a hand to her brow. Her bones seemed so fragile.

Finn examined her. 'Did you get injured?'

Maddie shook her head. 'I was lucky.' She laughed at herself then looked at Finn's bandaged hand. 'How are you?'

Finn held it up. 'Hurts like hell.' He put his hand to his chest. 'A cracked rib as well, nothing too serious.'

Maddie put her hand out and touched his chest where his heart was.

'I'm sorry I got you mixed up in this. I should be on a beach in Thailand by now.'

'Thailand?'

Maddie shrugged. 'Maybe, I don't know. I was going to head to Amsterdam from Edinburgh, then just see what flight left next. As long as it was far away from this dump. If you hadn't answered my call I don't know what I would've done. I needed a friend and you helped.'

She took his broken hand in hers and stroked the fingers, around the splint, over the discoloured and sunken knuckle.

Finn's phone buzzed again in his pocket.

'I need to go and see Ingrid,' he said.

But he didn't move, just let her hold his damaged hand.

'I'll be back soon,' he said. 'I'll bring food and the key to the main house, so you can get some rest.'

She kissed him on the lips.

'My saviour.'

17

Ingrid was in the hallway before he had the door closed behind him.

'Where have you been?'

Finn held up the two bags of shopping.

'Why didn't you answer your phone?'

'Battery died.' Finn moved past her into the kitchen.

'Jesus.' Ingrid shook her head. 'Have some sense, lad.'

'Sorry.'

'Think about what you've been through. I had no idea where you were.'

Something in her voice made Finn stop unpacking the groceries and turn. She was standing at the door with her hands at her face.

'I'm OK, Gran,' he said.

Ingrid rubbed at her hair. 'I thought I lost you last night. Do you understand? I heard about the crash, that folk were dead, and I thought you were one of them. Do you know what that felt like, after what happened with Sally?'

She sat down at the kitchen table and stared at her hands in her lap.

Finn stood there with a carton of milk in his hand. 'I saw that we were getting low on stuff so I went to the shop. Sorry, I should've left a note.'

Ingrid shook her head. 'We're not running out of anything.'

Finn came round to face her. 'I just needed some space to think.'

She reached out and touched his injured hand. 'I understand that but you have to be more considerate of those around you. I'm here to help, you know. So is Janet.'

Finn had to think for a minute who that was. Right, the counsellor.

'She's a good friend of mine,' Ingrid said. 'And she knows what she's doing. It's better to talk to her than just drive around thinking, churning things up in your mind.' She looked at him, the milk still in his hand. 'I can't imagine what it was like being in that aeroplane. I can't imagine what you saw but I want to help if I can.'

'I know.'

'Remember how it was with your mum. I don't think either of us could've got through that without each other.'

Ingrid's eyes were a startling blue even now, not dimmed by the years. She was a striking woman, must've been a heartbreaker when she was younger. Finn pictured Maddie wandering around the exhibits, picking up bones, flicking through guidebooks. She'd said she needed him. Sometimes that's all there is, people who need each other.

'I'll put this lot away,' Finn said, waving the milk.

Ingrid let go of his hand and he went back to the bags. He stole a glance at her as she stared out the window. The view could've been described as extraordinary except you got views just as spectacular all over Orkney. Rugged cliff tops, cascading waves, huge sweeps of sea and slabs of land, millions of years of slow war between them, the land trying to resist the expanses of water and retain its dignity against the onslaught. It felt like the roof of the world up here, the air thinner and purer, the land stronger, the elements more brutal. Like you were connected to the land in a way you couldn't be further south, as if the stuff of your bones was one with the earth, only separated by a fragile layer of skin. Finn imagined turning to stone, standing for thousands of years on the cliff, facing south, a warning to others.

Ingrid turned to him. 'How were the old guys?'

'What?'

'Before you went gallivanting you went to see them.'

The Tomb of the Eagles.

'They're fine.'

'Did they have much to say?'

A joke, of course, but something underneath that was half serious. The way she spoke about the remains, they weren't just a pile of bones. Ingrid sometimes talked as if they were still alive. Finn didn't believe that she actually heard voices, but she often said they spoke to her. He got it. Their presence, the continuity of it, gave you perspective on the dross of daily life. A feeling that whatever you were going through, someone went through the same thing in this spot thousands of years ago.

'They weren't so great with the advice today,' Finn said.

'Don't suppose they ever found themselves in quite your situation.'

Finn wondered about Ingrid. When he wasn't visiting she was alone, her husband and daughter dead and buried up the road. Sure, she had tourists in the summer and the Lewises along the way, but even for Orkney this place was isolated, the end of the road. She'd said that Janet was a good friend, but that was the first he'd heard of it.

He loved spending summers here growing up, mucking about on the farm, going on adventures in the fields, looking for old pottery, glassware or fossils. But those days seemed a lifetime ago. He had his own life, so where did that leave her?

He tried to imagine her funeral. Who would be there that Finn knew? He pictured himself standing over a hole in the ground at St Peter's, just him and the minister, the standing stone in the distance, surrounded by sea and sky.

'I wish Mum was here,' he said.

'Me too.'

'I went to see her on the way to the shop.'

Ingrid was silent for a moment. 'How's her stone?'

'Fine.'

'Angus's too?'

'Yeah.'

'Did you speak to her about what's happened?'

'A little.'

'She would be worried sick.'

'I know.'

Silence.

Eventually Finn spoke. 'How was Sally growing up?'

Ingrid considered this for a long time. 'A lot like you. Artistic, sensitive but headstrong. A little lost, too, I think.'

'How do you mean?'

Ingrid rubbed at a scratch on the tabletop. 'I don't think she really knew what to set her heart on, until you came along. She loved art, creating, but deep down I don't know if that drove her. She drifted through college, finding her way. When she fell pregnant she became much more focused, and when you were born, that was it. She found her purpose. Not all women want to be mothers, Finn, not by a long way, but she had it in her. I didn't expect that.'

Finn took a breath. 'Why did she never come back here? Why did she never ask for help?'

Ingrid smiled. 'Part of it was just her, bull-headed. I think she wanted to make a new home, start a family, do it on her own. I loved having you up here for holidays, but she wanted you and her to have your own place to call home, not rely on my generation for anything.'

'Did you ever fall out?'

Ingrid sat rubbing the table, flicking at the surface. 'We never did. I was so proud of her, I can't tell you.'

Finn looked around the kitchen. He'd sat here a hundred times before but it felt different, off kilter somehow.

'She wouldn't be proud of me,' he said.

Ingrid looked up. 'What do you mean?'

'All this. The plane. The dead folk.'

'Finn, she loved you, she would've supported you no matter what. Just like I will.'

'That's not good enough,' Finn said. 'There shouldn't need to be any "no matter what". That means I've fucked up.'

'You just need some help. We all need help sometimes.'

Finn noticed something on the floor behind Ingrid. His rucksack, the one that he had yesterday on the plane. He went round and picked it up.

'How did you get this?'

'It was in your bedside cabinet at the hospital.'

Finn unzipped it at the table. The George Mackay Brown

book at the top, a few of the pages bent over. He flicked through it.

'You still have that,' Ingrid said.

'Of course.'

'Sally loved it.'

Finn imagined his mum touching the cover, turning the pages, sighing at the end. 'Why did she name me after him?'

Ingrid shrugged. 'It's a nice Orcadian name. And he's a lovely character.'

'But he doesn't get what he wants in the end, to be a poet.'

'He lives a good life,' Ingrid said. 'That's enough.'

Finn dropped the book on the table and lifted his sketchbook out the bag. He remembered Maddie holding it, flicking, staring, smiling. The drawings all seemed to come from another time, drawn by a different hand, someone else entirely. He landed on some sketches of the gravestones at St Peter's, not plans for jewellery, just something for himself.

He took a tin of pencils from the bag and chose one then turned to a blank page. He tried to hold the pencil but the metal splint wouldn't let his outer fingers bend to support his thumb and index finger. He had no control. It was precarious and unsteady. He tried to draw a simple symmetrical shape, four loops on two sides like a butterfly, but the lines wobbled and the splint dragged along the page, smudging the whole thing and tearing at the paper. He closed his eyes and tapped the pencil against his forehead then dropped it on to the table and closed the notebook.

He opened his eyes to see Ingrid skinning up, pulling strands of grass apart and spreading them along a single Rizla, followed by a little sprinkle of Golden Virginia. She smoked a bit of weed on and off, a child of the sixties, something Finn discovered as a teenager. She licked along the gum and rolled it, no roach.

'Give me a draw,' Finn said.

She lit it and sucked in. 'You sure?'

Finn didn't usually smoke Ingrid's stuff but he wanted to now. He nodded, lifting his hand. 'Painkilling properties.'

Ingrid passed it to him and exhaled. He took a draw and handed it back, felt the rush to his head. He put his hand out and felt the grain of wood on the table.

There was a knock at the front door.

They exchanged a look. Ingrid cupped the joint in the palm of her hand and peered out of the window.

'It's that young policewoman.'

She carefully stubbed the joint out in an ashtray and lifted both into a high cupboard. She ushered Finn out of the kitchen and closed the door.

She blinked a couple of times then opened the front door. 'It's yourself.'

Linklater looked tired. Finn wondered if she'd had much sleep.

'Sorry to bother you, Mrs Sullivan,' Linklater said. 'But I need to speak to Finn again. Can I come in?'

'Of course.' Ingrid held the door open and Linklater stepped into the hallway. 'Go through.' Ingrid indicated the living room as she closed the door, Finn leading the way.

They stood in the middle of the room, Linklater waiting to be asked to sit. Finn loved this room as a kid, Ingrid's bookshelves brimming with secrets, the same with her racks of sixties and seventies rock albums. Finn used to spend hours wading through Thin Lizzy, AC/DC and Black Sabbath, absorbing the covers, the rough-hewn sounds. It never occurred to him that it was unusual having a gran into that stuff.

'What's this about?' Ingrid said. 'You spoke to the lad at the hospital.'

Linklater scratched at her neck. 'I'm afraid the situation has changed, we're now involved in a murder investigation.'

'You mean the people on the plane?' Finn said.

Linklater shook her head. 'I need you to confirm your whereabouts for all of yesterday, Finn, leading up to Kirkwall Airport at seven pm.'

Finn narrowed his eyes. 'Why?'

'He was here with me,' Ingrid said, moving into the room.

'That's right,' Finn said.

Linklater looked from one to the other. 'All day?'

Finn nodded.

'Did anyone else see you here?'

'No one came by,' Ingrid said. 'But you can take my word for it that he didn't leave the cottage until I took him to the airport. What's this about?'

'After getting no response at Mrs Pierce's house, we obtained a warrant and gained entry,' Linklater said. 'Kevin Pierce was dead inside, stabbed in the chest multiple times.'

18

He stood outside the visitor centre but didn't take the key out of his pocket. He rubbed at the skin under his eyes as if wiping something away, then stared at the door. It was once a tree and before that part of the earth and air, regenerated atoms. One day in the future it would be something else entirely, the molecules making up part of a worm or a bird or some animal that hadn't evolved yet. Finn leaned forward until his forehead was touching the door. He closed his eyes and breathed, the wind a constant force against his body.

Linklater had quizzed him some more about his movements, his reason for being on the island, his relationship to Maddie. He'd told her he had no relationship with her. He thought about that now. He hadn't given her up. He thought about that too. After Linklater left, Ingrid pushed him for information as well, echoing the cop.

Kevin Pierce. He wanted to know all about Kevin Pierce. What kind of man he was, what kind of husband.

Finn had waited for two hours after Linklater left. He didn't want to draw attention to himself leaving the house, didn't want to arouse Ingrid's suspicions. And anyway, he needed time to think it all through. He was tied to Maddie now. Ever since he saw her at airport security he'd been drawn into her orbit, had become tangled up in her. He touched his lips with his tongue and imagined that he could still taste her from their kiss earlier.

He could still give her up. Depending on how she was in a few moments' time, maybe he would. He'd be in the shit for lying and helping her, but maybe he had to untether himself from her if she was sinking and dragging him under.

He took the key out of his pocket and opened the door then walked down the hall, looking in the different display rooms. He went to the kitchenette. She was slumped at the table, her jacket folded underneath her head for a pillow. The bag of money was at her feet, the strap wrapped around both her legs. Her forearms were covered in large freckles. Her hair had fallen over her eyes and he lifted a strand and tucked it behind her ear. The sight of her face, relaxed and peaceful, made his stomach tight. He looked at her hands, bony knuckles with thin veins. He imagined those hands plunging a knife into a man's chest, the force needed to get through the ribs into the heart and lungs, the energy needed to pull it out and shove it back in, again and again. How many times had Kevin Pierce been stabbed? How hard did he try to defend himself? Didn't attackers get defensive wounds? Finn looked again at Maddie's hands, arms and face.

He took the seat across from her and shook her arm.

'Maddie.'

He wondered how much sleep she got last night in the cow-shed.

'Maddie, you need to wake up.'

She moaned and stirred then let out a heavy breath. She sat up with a grunt, blinked several times and recognised him. 'Hey.' She cricked her neck, stretched her arms up and arched her back. 'Jesus, how long was I asleep?'

Finn watched her movements, slow, groggy. 'Three hours.'

He glanced out of the window. The sun was setting over the western corner of the sea, a shimmer of high cloud diffusing the light, throwing orange and yellow streaks across the sky. Not even a whole day had passed since Maddie came into his life. Imagine what a lifetime with her would be like.

Maddie untangled herself from the seat and the bag. She lifted her mug from the table and headed to the kettle.

'Want one?' She switched it on and rubbed at her hips. Finn saw a flash of burgundy bra between the buttons of her blouse as she stretched.

'I need to talk to you about something,' he said.

Maddie glanced at her bag on the floor then back at Finn. She turned and threw a teabag into the mug.

'What?'

'Your husband.'

Maddie snorted. 'I don't want to talk about that arsehole.'

'He's dead.'

Maddie laughed. 'Don't be ridiculous.'

Finn watched her like an eagle tracking prey. He tried to read her body language, his eyes darting from her face to her hips, noting how she held herself.

'I'm serious.'

Maddie stopped moving. 'Don't mess with me.'

'Kevin is dead.'

Maddie shook her head. 'How would you know that?'

Finn stared, trying to make sense of her. This had to make sense.

'The cop I spoke to at the hospital,' he said. 'She came to Ingrid's cottage just now to speak to me. About your husband.'

'I don't follow.' Maddie ran her finger along the edge of the worktop.

'They went round to your house but there was no answer, so they got a warrant. They found him inside, stabbed to death.'

'Why are you saying this?' Maddie said, rubbing her forehead.

'Because it's true.'

She held on to the worktop with both hands, the rush of the boiling kettle behind her.

'Maybe you should sit down,' Finn said.

'I don't believe it.'

'Sit down, Maddie.'

She took several big breaths, but no tears came. Finn didn't know what he was expecting. She wandered to the table and slumped into the chair.

'This is bullshit,' she said under her breath. 'Some kind of weird game. The police are up to something.'

'Come on.'

She looked at him for the first time since he'd told her. 'Maybe they suspect you're in contact with me, and they want to flush me out with a lie.'

'That's ridiculous.'

Maddie shook her head.

Finn swallowed, felt his Adam's apple. 'I have to ask you something.'

'Don't bother,' she said. 'I didn't kill him, for Christ's sake. Do I look like a murderer?'

She had her hands out in supplication.

'Do you think these hands stabbed someone?'

'You seem angry,' Finn said, voice level.

'I am fucking angry,' Maddie said, running her hands through her hair. 'My husband got himself killed, and now I'm the main suspect.'

'I thought you might be sad.'

'Of course I'm sad. I mean I hated the cheating, bullying prick, but I didn't want him dead.'

Finn studied her. It seemed as if this was all news to her, but maybe she was just a good actor.

'You have to go to the police now,' he said.

'Are you crazy?'

'But they'll know you didn't do it. Forensics.'

'If you trust those idiots to get it right you've got a lot more faith in Orkney police than I do.'

'If you stay hidden it makes you look guilty.'

Maddie was wide-eyed. 'I already look guilty. I have a bag of Kev's money and I helped crash a plane rather than come back.'

That was the first time she'd said anything about guilt for the plane. He felt it too, deep in his bones, swimming in his blood.

He thought about what she'd said. A dead husband, a bag of money, her panic on the plane. What did it take to kill someone? Would it show on your face if you could do that? He stared at her now. Her head was gently shaking, eyes down at the table. He tried to picture her doing something like that to Kev. If she could do it once, she could do it again. He realised his fingertips were gripping the edge of the table.

'Tell me what happened at your place,' he said.

'I got in from work at the nursing home and found him screwing that stupid cow from behind on our bed. I turned around and left the house. I got the money from where it was hidden and headed to the airport.' She slapped the table. 'Claire, the bitch, you've got to go and see her.'

'Wait a minute.'

She reached out and took his hands.

'Go and speak to Claire.'

Finn pulled his hands away. 'And say what?'

'Ask her what happened after I left. She'll tell you I had nothing to do with Kev's death.'

Finn stared at her. 'Unless she did it and wants to blame you.'

'Why would she kill him? She could have had him for all I cared.'

'Maybe they had an argument after you left. Maybe he got violent. You said he was a bully, did he ever hit you?'

Maddie laughed. 'You want to see the bruises, would you believe me then?'

'Did you go to the police about it?'

Maddie shook her head.

'Why not?'

'That stuff is between husband and wife, behind closed doors, they're not interested.'

'So maybe that's what happened, maybe Claire was defending herself.'

Maddie thought for a moment. 'I don't believe she killed Kev.'

'Well, if you didn't and she didn't, who did?'

'Kev was into a lot of bad stuff. As well as the salvage scam and the deliveries, he was into some bullshit with the Sanderson brothers. God knows what else. I didn't want to know the details.'

Even Finn had heard of the Sanderson brothers, Kirkwall

thugs bringing in coke and heroin from Russia, according to pub rumour.

Finn glanced at the bag on the floor. 'Maybe losing a hundred grand didn't do him any favours.'

Maddie stared at the bag.

'Just a thought,' Finn said.

Maddie shook her head. 'No, the money was his, he didn't owe anyone.'

'You sure?'

She looked down at the floor. 'No.'

Finn pushed his chair back and stood up, hands on the edge of the table. 'You have to take all this to the police.'

'They'll just say I killed him, they won't care about anything else. They've got his body, me on the run, the wronged wife, the bag of money. It stinks.'

'It does.'

Maddie tilted her head and reached out but Finn was too far away. 'You believe me, right?'

'Would you believe me, if the situation was reversed?'

'I like to think I would.'

'I don't even know you, Maddie.'

'You know me as well as anyone. I felt it yesterday at the airport, I know you did too. You get me, we're the same.'

'We're not the same.'

'We were both leaving, escaping.'

'I wasn't escaping, I was going home.'

'To your girlfriend?'

'Leave Amy out of this.'

'Is that why you were chatting me up the whole time?'

'My relationship with her is nothing to do with this.'

'I know you want to fuck me.'

Finn laughed. 'Are you offering me sex to keep me on your side?'

'I'm not offering anything. And you're already on my side.'

Finn gave her a look and walked to the door. He glanced across the hall at the Neolithic exhibitions, the skulls and skeletons. He wondered if things were as complicated back in their day, if this kind of chaos came into their lives. He imagined being a corpse pegged out on the cliff, waiting for eagles and buzzards, seagulls and crows to come peck out his eyes, tear at his flesh, until he was nothing but a pile of windswept bones.

He turned back to Maddie. She was standing close enough that he could smell her, perfume and sweat, a vague stink from the cowshed, stress oozing from her pores. Behind her, the cup of tea she'd begun to make sat stewing.

'If you won't go to the police, I'll speak to them,' he said. 'I'll tell them to talk to Claire.'

Maddie had her hands on her hips. 'They'll know the information came from me, that we've been in contact since the crash. Then you'll be in trouble.'

'I can't get in any more trouble than I already am.'

'Think about it,' Maddie said. 'They presume we were both responsible for the plane. If they find out we've been together since then, why couldn't we have been together before yesterday as well?'

'But we weren't.'

'They don't know that. If they think we're working together, maybe we were both involved in Kev's death.'

'That's ridiculous, I've never met him, I don't even know where you live.'

'Do you think they care?' Maddie took a step closer. 'They've got a dead body and two people they already blame for the crash. It's not a big step to pin his death on us.'

'This is fucked up.'

Finn felt the doorframe against his back as Maddie stepped closer.

She spoke in a hushed voice. 'You've helped me so much. You've already saved me once. I needed you this morning and you came through. We have a connection, I know you feel it.'

She touched the button of his shirt. Finn looked at the hand, imagined it gripping a knife. The smell of her was in his nose now, musty and feral.

'Go and see Claire,' she said. 'Find out what happened. If we're going to sort this out we have to do it together.'

He thought she was going to kiss him again. He wanted her to, wanted much more than that. But she didn't lean in, she just stood looking at him with big eyes, her mouth straight, her hand on his chest feeling his heart under his shirt.

19

Finn edged the car along the winding lane of John Street. Stromness was just a handful of steep lanes straggling between Ferry Road and Back Road up the hill. To his left were the tiny vennels sloping down to the water, the tenement houses end-on to the sea, each with its own ancient jetty going back to fishing times. These days the town was mostly a ferry port, the huge MV *Hamnavoe* sitting in dock now, Finn catching glimpses of its monstrous white bulk down the alleyways as he drove.

The roads were built long before cars and there was no room for traffic to go both ways, no pavement either. But the system worked, mainly because no one ever came here. The shops were an odd mix of ancient brown places, unchanged in fifty years, and shinier blue and white properties turned into art galleries, workshops and cafes by recent incomers. Ageing hippies came here to find quiet and be inspired by the sea, making things out of flotsam and driftwood, painting unrealistically tranquil seascapes. Finn passed the Pier Arts Centre, closed for renovation. Seemed like the whole island shut down in winter. Sleet spattered the windscreen, the wipers smearing the slush into the corners as he crawled along.

In the window of a bric-a-brac shop he saw a police poster for Project Kraken, with a cartoon of a blue merman-beast on it. 'Protecting the waters of the Highlands and Islands,' it read. 'If you suspect it, report it,' then a number to call. Finn wondered if anyone ever phoned. That wasn't the way things were done around here. This far away from the centres of power, in this remote landscape, people had spent thousands of years doing things their own way, doing what they must to survive the harshness of the conditions. If someone was smuggling in bricks of dope or bags of pills, there were hundreds of miles of empty coastline to do it in, and who could blame them? If folk were out at night stripping the sunken fleet of copper and steel, taking valuables that might make a bit of money on the black market, fair play. If people were out poaching, as long as nobody got hurt, where was the harm? The idea of authority felt so remote here. The idea that you'd do something because people in Edinburgh or London told you to was ludicrous.

The winding road went over a mound and Finn saw the vast snowy humps of Hoy and Graemsay up ahead behind the fishing cottages. The sky was ominous, snow clouds tumbling over each other, the world darkening.

He reached his turn-off and smiled at the name of the street, Hellihole Road. One letter away from the worst address in the world. He indicated and turned. The street was like any other, short houses crouched against wind and rain, rough grey cladding and small windows, every feature designed to keep the outside from getting in, to achieve some semblance of warmth in the brutal northern winters.

He pulled over at number twelve and switched the engine off. He didn't have a plan. He'd chewed it over for the hour it took to get here. Stromness was almost as far away as you could get from Isbister in South Ronaldsay without heading to the outer isles. But he hadn't settled on an angle, hadn't decided how to play it. Maybe he should just go to the police, hand over responsibility. What Maddie said was true, he might be implicated, but so what? He felt screwed either way, so maybe just let the cards fall as they would.

A gust of wind rocked the car and Finn closed his eyes. He remembered sitting in the cabin, buffeted by turbulence, his hands tied together in his lap. He heard the screams of panic as the plane flipped and plummeted, nosedived to earth, then split. Saw the propeller crushing that old couple in their seats. Felt Maddie's kiss on his lips as she left him in the wreckage.

He got out of the car, again being careful with the door in the wind, and walked to the house. He rang the bell and waited. Spits of sleet were swept into his eyes by the wind and he wiped them away.

The door opened on the chain and a face peered out.

'Claire?'

'Who are you?'

'My name's Finn Sullivan, I need to speak to you.'

'It's not a good time,' she said, closing the door.

Finn put his foot in the gap between door and frame. 'I really need to talk to you.'

'Get your foot out of my door.'

'It's important.'

'It's really not a good time.' Claire kicked at his foot but she only had socks on.

'It's about Kevin Pierce.'

She stared at him. She was pretty in an obvious way, big lips in a natural pout, blue eyes. She was shorter than Maddie by a couple of inches, petite, packed into tight leggings and a running top. She was younger than Maddie too, closer to Finn's age, and she had on too much make-up, her eyebrows over-sculpted and fake-looking. What had Kevin seen in her that he hadn't got from his wife?

'I don't have anything to say about Kev,' Claire said. 'Now go away or I'll call the police.'

'I was thinking of calling them myself,' Finn said. 'They might be interested in what I know.'

'Piss off.' Claire looked beyond Finn down the street.

'I've been speaking to Maddie,' Finn said.

She narrowed her eyes. 'Who the hell are you?'

'Can I come in?'

She looked at him for a long time then shook her head.

'We talk here. If you move your foot I'll open the door properly. But we do it here, not inside.'

Finn moved his foot and she took the chain off the door.

'You've got one minute.'

Finn tried to see down the hall, if anyone else was about, but it was too gloomy inside. 'Like I said, I've been speaking to Maddie.'

'How? She's been missing since the crash, it's all over the news.'

Finn nodded. 'We met on the plane. We've kept in touch.'

'She's OK? The police said she might be dead.'

'She's fine.'

'Good,' Claire said. It seemed sincere.

'Maddie told me what you and Kevin were up to.'

'I don't know what you mean.'

'Yes you do, she caught the two of you together.'

Claire shook her head. 'That's bullshit.'

Finn watched her, looking for signs. 'Kevin's dead.'

She looked surprised, but then that's what she would do if she was covering something.

'Don't be ridiculous.' She looked along the street again, fingers tapping on the doorframe.

Finn nodded. 'The police told me. He was stabbed to death at home.'

'You're joking.'

Finn couldn't read her. Was she playing him? 'I'm deadly serious.'

'Jesus,' Claire said. 'Did Maddie do it?'

Finn angled his head. 'Why do you say that?'

Claire looked at him as if he was stupid. 'They're married, that's why. And she's missing after leaving on a plane. That's a bit suspicious.'

'She says you might've had something to do with it.'

Claire laughed but it sounded forced. 'Fuck off.' She began to close the door. 'This conversation is over.'

Finn's arm went out to stop the door.

'Get to fuck,' Claire said.

'Maddie said you were sleeping with Kev. She found you together. When she left for the airport, the two of you were still there, in her bed.'

'She's lost the plot. Maddie's always been a bit unhinged. Now she's just making all this shit up. To be honest the quicker she gets found the better. You should tell the police where she is and be shot of her.'

She was right, this was none of his business, not really. And yet.

'She doesn't seem unhinged to me,' Finn said.

'Do you mean before or after you were in a plane crash with her?'

The sleet was falling heavier now, Finn getting damp patches on his shoulders. 'Can we please go inside? I'm sure we can sort this out.'

'Are you kidding? You come here and accuse me of having an affair and killing someone?'

'I'm not accusing you of anything.'

'It sounds like you are.'

'I just need to know what happened.'

'It's pretty obvious what happened. Maddie lost the plot, killed Kev and ran away. She didn't manage to escape and now she's playing you, shifting the blame to me. It's bullshit.'

Finn stared at her. Claire avoided eye contact.

'What happened between you and Maddie?' he said.

'How do you mean?'

'She said you used to be best friends.'

A look flickered across her face, maybe a hint of regret, maybe anger.

'Things change.'

'Over a guy?'

Claire snorted. 'Ask Maddie since you're best mates all of a sudden.'

Something caught her eye down the street and she shrank into the house.

Finn took his hand away from the door and turned. Walking towards them was a tall man with a gelled parting, hair buzzed to the skin at the sides, stubble and narrow eyes. He was in an FCUK T-shirt and jeans, body tight underneath, army tattoos up his forearms and biceps.

'Hey babe,' he said to Claire. 'Who's this clown?'

Claire's body tensed. 'He's collecting for charity.'

The guy looked Finn up and down. 'Where's your clip-board?'

Finn looked at Claire, then nodded past the guy. 'Left it in the car.'

'What charity?'

'Macmillan Cancer Care.'

The guy looked at Claire, as if trying to puzzle something out. He turned back to Finn. 'We're not interested, so be a good boy and piss off.'

Finn looked back at Claire as he spoke. 'Sorry to have bothered you.'

'No worries,' Claire said.

'And don't come back when I'm not here,' the guy said. 'My wife's a soft touch. If I find out she's given you anything, you'll be in trouble.'

'No problem,' Finn said, and walked to the car.

The guy took hold of Claire's arm and guided her further into the house. He stood on the step and watched as Finn got in the car and started the engine. He was still there when Finn looked in the rear-view mirror and turned on to Back Road, heading home.

20

Finn flicked the indicator and turned off the main road at Stenness. He drove past the first spread of standing stones and kept on the lane across the tiny isthmus of land between the lochs of Stenness and Harray. He got to the Ring of Brodgar and pulled into the car park opposite. His was the only car there. Brodgar was one of Orkney's biggest tourist attractions in the summer, colossal standing stones arranged in a circle amongst heather and bracken. It was so well preserved it looked like something from a fantasy movie set, and Finn imagined a pagan sacrifice, cloaked disciples bowing down to the first rays of sun filtering through the ring.

With the weather closing in and the exposed moorland flanked by brackish water on both sides, Brodgar had a forbidding air about it, something menacing in the gloom. A flock of oystercatchers lifted out of the heather as he trudged towards the stones, their orange beaks daggers of colour in the grey sky. More sleet was coming in from the west, the sky dappled over there. It would be here in a few minutes.

He stopped at the first stone and put his hand against it, felt its rough bulk. It was fifteen feet high, the width of a man, God knows how many tons. Finn wondered about the people who brought it here, the effort involved. The logistics of digging deep holes, cutting the stones, transporting them. He vaguely remembered that they used logs to roll them from wherever they came from, but there were no trees on Orkney any more. All that hard graft. Was it for the gods? Sunrises and sunsets, all the solstice stuff, why did they think it was so important? Maybe they sought protection from the vagaries of existence, a guarantee of a good harvest, healthy children, long life. Good luck with that, Finn thought. The truth was that the mightiest sun god in the world wasn't going to save them, they were on their own. And looking for answers in the sky was pointless, worse than pointless because it gave you false hope, made you believe everything would be OK. The reality was that bad things just happen, and you can do nothing about it.

Claire had been hiding something, Finn was sure. Did she already know that Kevin was dead? Everyone likes to think they can read people, but it's crap. Going with your gut is wrong just as often as it's right. What was his instinct now? He didn't even know. The oystercatchers circling the loch knew about instinct, they acted on it without thinking. He was cursed with free will, the ability to think.

He felt a spatter of sleet as clouds swept overhead. He got on his knees in the wet gorse, his hand still touching the ancient stone. He put his other hand on it, tried to feel its rhythm, its connection to the earth, the universe, the people who had put it there all those years ago. Dampness soaked into his jeans as he closed his eyes. He wondered what it looked like to anyone driving past, a deluded hippy kid praying to old gods amongst a bunch of rocks in the middle of nowhere. Give me an answer, he said to himself, aware of how stupid it was but not even caring. Tell me what to do, oh great ones.

His phone rang.

He pushed himself up, rubbed his hands together then pulled out his phone.

'Hey, Ingrid.'

'Just checking in with my favourite grandson. Making sure you're OK.'

Her voice was too light, forced.

The sleet was getting heavier. Finn raised his face skywards, felt the wetness on his skin. 'I'm fine.'

'You can do whatever you want, Finn, you're a grown-up. But if you're going to take the car at least check with me first. I might've needed it.'

'Sorry.'

'I've had someone round to speak to you. The young reporter from the *Orcadian*, the one who was at the hospital. Her name is Freya.'

'What did you say?'

'Sent her away with a flea in her ear. Told her she should get a job that didn't involve harassing people.'

'Thanks.'

Finn heard a bird call and looked left. A lone curlew stalked through the heather, jabbing its sharp curved beak into the undergrowth.

'I'm just heading home,' he said.

He heard the beep for another call on his phone.

'Hang on a minute, Gran.'

It was Amy.

The curlew sensed something and took off, away from the incoming weather.

'It's Amy, Gran, I'd better get it.'

He took the call. 'Hey.'

'Hi, honey, how's it going?'

The sleet was harder now, almost hail, stinging Finn's face and the hand holding the phone. He huddled behind a standing stone and sheltered from the wind.

'Fine.'

'How are you feeling?'

She meant physically, he presumed, or maybe more than that. Where to start?

'I'm OK, a few aches and pains but nothing some painkillers can't sort out.'

'Go easy,' Amy said. 'You know.'

Those last two words, freighted with meaning. A while after his mum had died, when he was already together with Amy, Finn had begun taking some prescription opiates he found at the back of the bathroom cabinet. Just to smooth the edge off the sadness to begin with. But he soon got used to life with no edges and kept taking them. His doctor was a dowdy middle-aged woman who'd known Sally. She had two teenage sons of her own and was overflowing with empathy, so Finn played little orphan boy for all he was worth, got repeat prescriptions without any hassle. Before long he was smothering himself in the fog of it, to the point where it affected his life, his ability to communicate. It turned out that life with no edges wasn't much of a life at all, but Finn didn't care enough to change by himself. Amy stepped in and sorted it. Nothing dramatic, no big intervention, just a quiet word, a promise of help, careful monitoring, a gradual reduction in the amount he was taking over weeks until he was free of it and able to go to the shops and come back with the correct groceries. That was his girlfriend, quiet and efficient, good and decent, honest and caring.

He tried to remind himself of that.

'It's nothing like before,' Finn said. 'Just helps with the pain.'

'Where are you? Sounds windy.'

'Brodgar.'

'Remember last time?'

Finn smiled. 'It's not exactly the weather for that.'

They'd come up here in the summer, stayed with Ingrid for a week, did all the tourist stuff that Finn knew back-to-front from childhood visits. It was refreshing seeing it all through Amy's eyes, discovering the spirit of the place all over again. They drove out here at night, midsummer sky still light, and lay down in the heather inside the stone circle, looking at the stars. They made love in the middle of the circle, joking about it afterwards, giving themselves up to ancient spirits. Only five months ago, but it felt like forever.

'What are you doing there?' Amy said.

'Getting wet.'

'Apart from that.'

'Clearing my head.'

Amy coughed and Finn sensed a change of gear. 'I'm coming to see you.'

'There's no need, I'm fine.'

'That's not the point,' Amy said. 'I want to be there for you.'

'There's nothing you can do here.'

'There's no point trying to talk me out of it,' Amy said. 'What am I going to do here, sit on my arse and twiddle my thumbs? What if you're not allowed off the island before Christmas? I'm coming tomorrow.'

'Amy, there's no point.' His voice was feeble.

'It's already sorted,' Amy said. 'They've opened the airport so I'm flying up. I couldn't get on today's flight, the girl on the phone said half the world's media is on it. Even more reason for me to be there.'

'Amy, I need to get out of here, the weather's closing in.'

'I love you, babe.'

'Love you, too.'

Finn put his phone away and wiped the wetness from his face. He pictured Amy lying naked underneath him in the middle of the circle. He felt ashamed. He placed his forehead against the standing stone, communing with the gods, then turned towards the car. As he walked, he scanned the sky for oystercatchers but they'd flown east, escaping the incoming storm.

21

He parked at the visitor centre and got out. He'd outrun the weather for now and the sky over the firth was grey but dry, the clouds just a high smear. The wind was still a force, it would drag the rain this way soon enough.

Before he reached the front door he heard the sound of a car engine. He turned and saw a blue Ford pull up next to Ingrid's car. A young woman unfolded herself from the driver's seat like a waking insect. She was six foot tall and gangly, big eyes and a sharp nose framed by a severe black bob. She was dressed like a kid playing office dress-up, mismatched jacket and skirt, huge canvas tote bag slung over her shoulder. Finn thought of Maddie inside with the holdall.

'Mr Sullivan?' the woman said.

She saw the face Finn made. 'I know, you don't want to talk to me, blah blah blah. I get it. I've already had a run-in with your lovely grandmother so I know the Sullivan script off pat.'

'Then you know I have nothing to say.'

Finn couldn't work out what to do with his body. He'd been reaching for the door handle when she arrived. Now he shifted away from the house, aware of who was inside. He wanted to lead the reporter away from the building, but that would seem weird. He should get back in the car and go to Ingrid's, but then the reporter would wonder why he'd come here.

'You have a story whether you like it or not,' she said. 'You are the story, you and this missing woman. You're at the centre of a media storm.'

Finn looked around at the view beyond the cliff. 'I thought the centre of a storm was supposed to be calm.'

'You know what I mean. Hey, I didn't introduce myself, I'm Freya Magnusson, reporter with the *Orcadian*.'

She rifled through her bag and produced a card, handed it to him. He looked at it but didn't take it.

'Go on,' Freya said. 'It might come in handy.'

'I doubt it.'

'Roach material, if nothing else.' She raised her eyebrows as if sharing a joke and prodded the card at him. He took it and put it in his pocket.

'You're in quite a situation,' she said.

Finn wondered how much she knew. 'Am I?'

Freya tilted her head. 'It's not every day we have a plane crash in Orkney with multiple deaths. This is the biggest thing that's happened here since someone spotted the longships on the horizon twelve hundred years ago. And I'm here to report on it.'

So she didn't know about Kevin yet.

'Go away,' Finn said.

He had his back to the building and imagined curtains twitching.

'I could go away,' Freya said. 'I already have an eyewitness account of the crash. Spoke to Charlotte the stewardess this morning. She had a lot to say about the behaviour of some of the passengers, if you know what I mean.'

A gust of wind made them both steady themselves. Freya nodded at the door. 'Maybe we could discuss it inside?'

'No.'

'Why are you here, anyway? It's not open this time of year.'

'We look after the place while the owners are away. Just keeping an eye on it.'

'So we can't go into the warm, non-windy building to talk?'

'No.'

She moved closer. She was wearing chunky heels that made her taller than him. She dropped her voice. 'Mr Sullivan, Finn. I'm going to write this article whether you speak to me or not. This is a great opportunity for me. We're even printing a special edition. There isn't a paper due for four days but this fell into our laps and we need to move fast. I can run the story with what I have, quotes from Charlotte, rescue workers, air traffic control and the police.'

She paused.

'You can imagine that scenario doesn't make you look good. Or I could use your side of it as well, balance it out. I'm sure you have good reasons for what happened up there.'

'It wasn't my fault.'

'That's exactly what our readers need to hear. If they can see the real you, so much the better.'

'I'm not speaking to you, end of discussion.'

Freya stuck out her bottom lip. 'Have you any idea where Mrs Pierce is?'

'No comment.'

'How long have you known her?'

'No comment.'

'Did she tell you she was married?'

'No comment.'

'Do you think she's alive or dead?'

'No comment.'

'Did she tell you why she was leaving her husband?'

'What makes you think she was leaving her husband?'

Freya smiled. 'It works both ways. You tell me something, I tell you something.'

'No deal.'

Freya sighed. 'Have it your way, but you know they've opened the airport.'

'So?'

'The muckrakers from the *Sun*, *Record*, *Mail* and the rest of the gutter will be here soon. You think they'll be sympathetic to your side?'

'I couldn't give a shit.'

'That's good,' Freya said, smiling. 'You keep that up. I hope it works out for you, I really do.'

'You talk a lot for a reporter. I thought you were supposed to listen to people for a living.'

Freya cupped her hands to the sides of her head. 'I'm all ears.'

Finn felt a buzz in his pocket and pulled his phone out. A text from Maddie:

Get rid of her.

He put his phone away, trying not to look at the building behind him.

'Bad news?' Freya said.

'Just Ingrid wondering where I am.' Finn moved towards his car.

'I like Ingrid,' Freya said. 'We have a lot in common.'

'Yeah?'

She touched his arm as he unlocked the car with a beep.

'We both have your best interests at heart.' Her voice was serious.

Finn opened the car door and Freya took a step back.

'I thought you were going to check on that place,' she said, nodding at the visitor centre.

'I'll do it later. Better see Ingrid.'

Freya looked at the windows of the building, then back at Finn. 'I might stay and have a look around.'

'Please leave.'

Freya weighed that up and glanced out to sea. 'Amazing views from here. Lovely day for a clifftop walk.'

'Just go.'

'I'm only messing, I'm on a deadline. The story of the century won't write itself.' She bounded towards her car and turned as she reached it. 'You've got my contact info, do yourself a favour and use it. Sooner rather than later.'

Finn shook his head and watched as she spun the Ford around and out the gate. He kept his eyes on the car as it bumped along the track through the fields, up the hill and out of sight. He rested his head on the roof of Ingrid's car and felt the shock of cold metal against his skin. He listened to his own breathing, felt his body ache and counted to ten.

22

The door was locked and he'd left her the key, so he knocked. He remembered a little pretend gang he'd had at primary school with two girls, Emily and Nina. He'd always been more friendly with girls when he was younger, only starting to hang out with boys when puberty hit, no real clue about how boys interacted with each other. The gang had a secret knock that he could still remember now. He imagined using it on the visitor centre door and being transported back to a time before all this.

The door clicked open and he slid inside. He smelt alcohol on her breath as she closed the door behind him.

'You've been drinking,' he said.

'I needed to relax.'

There was a sway to her body and she blinked slowly as she spoke.

'Where did you get booze?' Finn said.

Maddie waved at the connecting door to the Lewises' home. It was open with the key in the lock. 'They have a decent drinks cabinet. Care to join me?'

Finn took the key out of the lock. He'd meant for her to have a wash and a rest, not this. 'You shouldn't be going through their stuff.'

Maddie frowned at him.

'Make a note of everything you take or touch,' he said. 'I'll need to put it back the way it was.'

She walked past him into the Lewis house. He followed. He'd been in here before when the Lewises were around, of course, but he'd also sneaked through on his own in the past, on previous stays with Ingrid. He would offer to check the centre, then once inside he would turn the key in the adjoining door and wander around their private space, lifting a picture off the mantelpiece, looking through a drawer or two, imagining their lives. Nothing sinister, just the inquisitive instinct of a child, the urge to spy on someone else's world.

So he knew where everything was, the TV remote control and the steak knives, the shampoo and the old-people underwear drawer. Mr and Mrs Lewis never had kids so they'd thrown all their energy into the tomb, building it up from a hole in the ground to a thriving business. They had plenty of money in the bank but hadn't decorated their chintzy house in thirty years, all floral curtains and shagpile carpet.

'We shouldn't be through here,' Finn said.

Maddie headed for the sideboard where a bottle of Bombay Sapphire sat on top. 'I'll make you one.'

She glugged gin into two glasses then went to the kitchen. Finn heard the fridge open and close, then the freezer, then she came back in and handed him a drink.

'There's no lime, but I found ice.'

The cubes chimed in the glasses as they clinked and sipped. The taste made Finn flash back to the airport lounge.

'What did she want?' Maddie said.

'Who?'

'The girl with the goofy face.'

'She writes for the *Orcadian*. Wants my story, about the crash.'

'Does she know about Kev?'

'No, but she will soon.'

'Then what?'

Finn had intended to sip his gin but he looked at the glass and it was almost finished.

'What did Claire say?' Maddie said.

'She denied everything, said she didn't know Kevin was dead.'

'You believed her?'

'She seemed genuine.'

'She's a good liar when she needs to be, I found that out the hard way.'

Finn wondered if the same applied to Maddie. He narrowed his eyes. 'How did you two become friends?'

Maddie drank. 'What do you mean?'

'You don't seem very alike, that's all.'

She looked at him. 'You don't know me and you don't know her.'

'So tell me.'

Maddie waved a hand at nothing. 'I don't know, proximity, I guess. There's not exactly a lot going on in Stromness most nights. We met at the bar in the Royal one night. Kev and Lenny already knew each other, so we all just fell together.'

'Wait,' Finn said. 'Lenny is Claire's husband?'

'Didn't I say that already?'

'The same Lenny that Kev was running the salvage thing with?'

'Of course.'

'And you never thought to tell me?'

Maddie frowned. 'I thought I did.'

'I met him, at their house.'

Maddie finished her drink. 'How was he?'

'Aggressive.'

'Sounds right.'

Finn shook his head. 'This is a mess. I still think you should go to the police.'

'And tell them what?'

'The truth.'

Maddie went to pour another drink. She was standing at the window now, the sea view behind her. If Ingrid or Freya or anyone walked round this side of the house, she'd be visible. A crow glided past, riding the wind over the water.

'They won't believe me,' Maddie said. 'We've been through this.'

Finn handed her his empty glass and watched as she poured him another. Her hand was unsteady. How many had she had?

He went to the kitchen and came back with the tonic and ice. He finished the drinks off and they picked them up but didn't clink this time. The rush of the wind outside was a faint tremble in here, clouds racing east out the window. The hail he'd outrun at Brodgar would be here any minute.

'What are we doing, Maddie?' he said.

'What do you mean?'

Finn waved around at the ceramic dolphins on a shelf, the frilly lamp, the matching easy chairs.

'What's the plan? We can't go on like this.'

He realised that she didn't have the bag of money with her for the first time since they met. She must've hidden it somewhere in the house.

'You have to get me off Orkney,' she said.

Finn breathed through his nose. 'How? You can't get on a plane.'

'Boat.' She put her glass down and touched her hand to his arm.

'They'll be watching the ferries,' Finn said. 'And I can't leave the island so I can't smuggle you in the car boot.'

'Not like that,' she said, stroking his arm.

Finn looked at her hand then her eyes, misty with alcohol.

'I'll tell you later,' she said.

She took his hand and placed it on her breast. Finn could feel her heart underneath, and her scent filled his nose. She put her hand to his crotch and squeezed through his jeans until he became hard.

'You can't just . . .'

She stretched up and kissed him, long, her tongue deep in his mouth. She pulled away and placed a finger on his lips.

He was stroking her breast as she pushed against him.

'I want you,' she said. 'Inside me. Now.'

He thought of the bodies piled up in the hospital mortuary in Kirkwall, the dead passengers and crew. He thought of Kevin lying in a pool of his own blood at home. He thought about Maddie and the money, the crash and the police and the journalist and everything he'd let himself slide into without fighting. But he didn't stop, just kept going, letting himself sink further into Maddie.

23

'You are out of your mind,' he said.

He tried to give her a serious look but his eyes moved down her body, her breasts, stomach, the dark hair beneath. She was darker-skinned than Amy, more curvy, and her eyes just killed him.

'My face is up here,' she said, a deliberate echo of their first meeting. She kissed him and ran a finger down his body then along his cock. He felt it stir in response.

'Don't,' he said but he didn't mean it. 'You're crazy.'

She shook her head. 'It's the only way.'

'I'm not doing it.'

Her hand stopped on his cock and she flicked at the head.

'Ow,' he said.

'Then I'll do it myself.'

Finn looked round. They'd made it to the Lewises' bedroom, just, and fallen on to the flowery duvet while pulling at each other's clothes, pain shooting up Finn's arm from his hand as he struggled to get his T-shirt over his head, more pain across his chest as he stretched. She pushed him on to his back and hauled at his jeans and shorts then unpeeled her bra and slid her trousers and panties off. She straddled him, already wet, and guided him inside, her hair falling over her face, breasts moving as Finn reached for them. She came, collapsing on top of him, breathless, the smell of gin and sweat, and he flipped them both over, kept thrusting until her nails dug into his buttocks and he came inside her.

Now here they were, a damp patch on the duvet between them, little ornamental seals on the bedside cabinet staring at them.

Finn looked from the ornaments to her. 'You're going to take your husband's boat and sail it to mainland Scotland.'

'Yeah.'

'What kind of boat?'

'A wee thing with a cabin and an outboard motor.'

'And you're going to take it across the Pentland Firth, one of the most dangerous stretches of water in Europe, in the middle of winter.'

'What else can I do?'

Finn shook his head. 'Anything but that.'

'There isn't anything else. I need your help.'

'No way.'

'At least take me there. I can't get to the boat unless you drive me. You don't have to do anything else, no one needs to know we've been in touch. Just drop me at the boat and I'll take it from there.'

'Do you have any experience in boats?'

'I'll work it out.'

'You'll die on the firth.'

'I'll be fine.'

'You need maps, GPS, distress flares.'

'They're on the boat, I think.'

'You think?'

'Kev used it all the time for salvage and that was at night so it's obviously possible.'

'It's different taking a boat out in the shelter of Scapa Flow if you're experienced.'

'I don't have any option.'

'Go to the police.'

Maddie sat up and turned away. 'Let's not go through that again.'

Finn ran a finger down her spine. He thought of the bones in the tomb up the road, imagined a Stone Age man doing the same thing to his wife thousands of years ago.

'You think you can just fuck me and I'll do whatever you want?' he said.

He felt her body stiffen and she flinched from his touch. She picked her panties off the floor and pulled them on, then her jeans. She didn't bother with her bra, just whipped her blouse over her head and pulled her hair back into a ponytail.

'Is that what you think this is?'

'Isn't it?' He felt vulnerable, lying naked on the bed, now that she was dressed.

'Fuck you,' Maddie said.

'You just did.'

She walked out of the room in her bare feet. Her socks, boots and bra lay on the floor like bits of discarded lizard skin. He threw his clothes on and went after her, found her at the drinks cabinet fixing another gin.

'Maddie.'

He touched her shoulders and realised she was crying. She whipped round and threw a punch at his chest, then another. Both hits screamed in his body and he felt a pop at his ribcage. His hands went to his sides.

'I wish I'd never met you,' she said.

'Come on.'

She stepped back and wiped her nose. 'Ever since I laid eyes on you people have been dropping dead around us. You're a curse. Yesterday morning my life was shit, but at least I knew what to expect. Then I walked in on Kev and Claire and decided that was it. Even then, I thought I knew what I was doing. But now look at me.'

'Take it easy.'

She fixed him with a stare. 'Don't you dare say I fucked you so that you'd do what I want. I did it because I wanted to, because I'm scared and lonely and don't know what the hell to do.'

'Come here.' He pulled her into a hug, sobs against his chest, throbbing pain through him, his hands at her back. He closed his eyes and smelt her hair.

She lifted her head up. 'I can't stop thinking about the plane. Every time I close my eyes the cabin is breaking apart, you're back there, I'm up front, and I think it's the end. We fell out of the sky, Finn, we fell out of the sky and lived. Sometimes I wonder if that means something.'

'I know.'

'But it doesn't mean anything, it's just luck. Why did the others die and not us? I don't deserve to live ahead of them.'

'It's not a matter of deserving it.'

'I'm not so sure.'

'It's just chance.'

Maddie looked at him and something flitted across her face, something like shame. 'I'm glad it was them and not us. Isn't that terrible?'

'No.'

Her voice lowered. 'I feel like I can do anything now. We lived, we're indestructible. I know it sounds crazy, but if anyone can understand it's you. You understand, don't you?'

'I understand.'

24

He stood with a skull in his hand, aware of what it looked like if anyone could see him. Not that anyone would be around at this time of night, this time of year, way out here.

The Tomb of the Eagles was freezing, his fingers numb as he replaced the skull next to its compadres. He thrust his hands into his pockets and stamped his feet to get the blood flowing. On the walk up here in the dark he'd been pummelled by the westerly and imagined himself being carried over the cliff into the sky, blissfully swept into the upper reaches of the atmosphere above the clouds where aeroplanes still flew, criss-crossing the planet with their vapour trails.

He had told Maddie he was heading back to Ingrid's but instead had turned right when he left the Lewis place. He needed quiet and this was the quietest place he knew. The torch on his phone threw a thin beam of light up from where he'd placed it, enough to see by, but the corners of the cairn were shrouded in darkness. He pictured the dead rising, zombified bodies of the seven crash victims clawing their way out of the gloom towards him, dragging their feet and moaning. Each one a husband, father, wife, mother, daughter or son to someone. Each person leaving the deepest hole where their life had been, an absence as shocking as any explosion.

Finn kicked at the floor and disturbed some dirt. He coughed, his lungs straining in pain. The cough escalated, he couldn't shake it out, each new spasm making more daggers slide between his ribs. His mouth filled as he coughed something up, then spat it on the floor. He grabbed his phone and pointed the torch at the ground. There was darkness amongst the phlegm. Blood. Had they mentioned that in hospital? Maybe he hadn't escaped death after all, maybe death was stalking him, waiting for its chance to take him like the others. Perhaps he and Maddie were on borrowed time, the whole thing a chain reaction that would still claim them both.

He thought about Maddie's idea to steal the boat and sail it across the firth. He couldn't picture it, but then he couldn't picture saying no to her either. The more he thought about her the less he understood. Maybe she killed her husband and took the money. And yet Finn had just screwed her in his neighbours' bedroom. Maybe she walked away from the dying and injured on the airfield, yet he went to the cowshed and saved her, hid her from the police, from everyone.

His phone rang. Ingrid. Her fourth call in the last two hours. Always wondering where he was. He didn't blame her, he would be the same in her position. But he didn't answer the call. The truth was, he didn't know what to say to her.

*

'Switch it off,' Ingrid said.

But Finn couldn't. He sat forward in his seat watching Sky News, unable to look away. The glossy young presenter was in the car park of Kirkwall Airport, the runic lettering of the terminal building behind her. The crash story would've been enough to bring them here and keep them for a couple of days anyway, but the mysterious and beautiful missing woman, that was much more newsworthy. Only Finn knew that she had walked away unharmed. At the moment they were still just describing her as unaccounted for, but something in the tone of the reporting suggested they suspected. One of the air crash investigators held a press conference explaining that if a body had been thrown clear during the crash, it was highly unlikely they wouldn't have found it by now. The possibility had been raised of Maddie leaving the scene and the investigator hadn't ruled it out. He was a reedy man in a short-sleeved shirt, buttoned-down collar, thin oblong glasses. The press jumped on his refusal to deny it and ran with the idea of a hunt, the search for a pretty young woman, possibly injured or suffering from amnesia, in the vicinity of the airfield.

There was a lot of space in Orkney. The police had brought in reinforcements from mainland Scotland and roped in half the population of Kirkwall to trek through the adjoining fields searching for Maddie as well as wreckage. It was as if the world needed to find her to make sense of it all. She was the missing piece of the puzzle, the resolution they needed for the crash to finally go away, so they could move on to the next terrible trauma that the world would throw at them. But Maddie was no missing jigsaw piece, no easy closure, Finn knew that.

And then there was the media's treatment of Finn. The BBC, ITV and Sky hadn't found him on South Ronaldsay yet, but it was only a matter of time. The tabloids would be here first, the girl from the *Orcadian* was right. They would rip him to shreds because everyone loves a scapegoat. Finn, the fist-fighter on the plane, the abuser of the crew, would fit perfectly.

He gleaned from the coverage that Sean Bayliss was still in an induced coma. Charlotte the stewardess had returned home from hospital. She was said to have suffered severe shock. The presenter named her as Charlotte Woodside. Finn looked around the room for his rucksack, spotted it on the floor in the corner. He heaved out of his seat and over to it, pulled out his notebook, a pencil and the Mackay Brown novel. He sat back down with a sigh and opened the notebook. He went to a clean page and tried to write 'Charlotte Woodside' but the splint on his knuckle made it impossible to lean his hand on the paper, so his fingers hovered over the page like a nervous insect. He wrote slowly, a wobbly scrawl that he could only just make out. He went through the same process writing down 'Sean Bayliss'. He had to keep a note of their names.

He flicked back through the notebook, looking at the sketches he'd done at Brodgar and Skara Brae. Further back in the notebook were detailed drawings of some of the jewellery pieces he'd been working on for the degree show. Brooches and bracelets, delicate stuff with stones reflecting the colour palette of the islands, simple silver settings, slight nods towards runic text in the curve of the shapes, a hint of the past in what were supposed to be modern pieces. He thought about the stuff he'd been making back in Dundee. He'd been on course for graduating well, had a lot of things nearly finished for the end-of-year show, but what now? At least six weeks for his hand to heal, that's what the doc said. And that was just to get the splint off, then there would be stiffness in the knuckle, across the fingers, maybe physio, scar tissue under the surface. He thought about the way he used his jewellery instruments. There was no chance he'd be able to finish what he'd started making in time. And that was just the physical side of it. At the moment, he couldn't even imagine having the will to complete the work. Everything from before the crash seemed ghostly now, faded grey shadows of a life he used to lead. In comparison, everything since that night seemed too bright and vivid. Colours saturated his mind's eye when he thought about Maddie. Life was too loud now, too real to be thinking about going back to who he was and what he did before.

He closed the notebook and looked at the Mackay Brown book. Maddie had touched it at the airport lounge. It had been through the plane crash with him, and he felt like that had sullied it, destroyed its purity somehow. A simple story about a dreamer kid who preferred stories to real life. He wished he were more like Thorfinn in the book, conjuring up fictional worlds to escape into. By the end of the book, though, his namesake had given up writing stories and was content to just live, to exist in the world and be a part of humanity, linking what went before with what was to come. Finn tried to imagine himself settling down with Amy, with Maddie, with some unknown woman, faceless in his imagination, formless in his mind.

There was nothing on the news yet about Kevin Pierce. It would be unbearable when the police released that information. Imagine how the hunt for Maddie would escalate once they knew her husband had been murdered.

Finn rubbed his eyes and felt exhaustion sweep over him. All this chewing things over wasn't going to change anything. He had to act. But that presupposed he knew what to do.

The television was now showing a different glossy woman standing outside St Magnus Cathedral in the centre of Kirkwall. It looked bitterly cold. A few members of the public were there too, lined up for soundbites. The presenter spoke to the first person, a stocky, middle-aged woman Finn didn't recognise.

'Grace,' Ingrid said. 'She should know better.'

Finn couldn't focus enough to listen to Grace. The usual platitudes about tragedy, no doubt, inane stuff that filled air-time on news channels these days.

Glossy Presenter moved on to the next soundbite then the next, then walked to the doorway of the kirk and let the camera look inside. Dozens of people were milling about and holding candles, and the woman mentioned a vigil. She said it would go on through the night until tomorrow's memorial service for the seven dead. Finn listened closely but she didn't say the names of the deceased. He turned to Ingrid, who was sitting with her knitting on her lap, staring at her hands.

'They're having a memorial service?' he said.

'Don't get any ideas.'

'What do you mean?'

She gave him a sympathetic look. 'You can't go, Finn.'

'Why not?'

Ingrid raised her eyebrows at the television. Glossy Presenter had stepped back outside and was wrapping up her report, gliding away from the old stonework and furrowed brows inside.

'You know why not,' Ingrid said. 'The world's media will be there.'

'So?'

'You're not naïve, don't pretend to be. They'll crucify you.'

'I've done nothing wrong.'

He thought of Maddie at the visitor centre. He imagined he could still taste her on his tongue.

'They blame you,' Ingrid said. 'There will be relatives there.'

'I have to go.'

'Don't you dare.'

Finn sat upright. 'If I don't, it looks like I don't give a shit. That's worse.'

'Do you give a shit?' Ingrid said.

That stopped him in his tracks. 'What?'

'You've been acting very strange.'

Finn laughed. 'I was in a plane crash, Gran.'

'I just don't think you're in the right frame of mind for this.'

'What frame of mind should I be in?' Finn said.

Ingrid picked up her knitting. 'You have a meeting with Janet at eleven tomorrow morning.'

Finn rubbed at his forehead. 'Who the hell is Janet?'

Ingrid began the click-clack of her needles. 'The counsellor. She spoke to you in hospital.'

'Christ, I'm not going to that.'

'Yes, you are.'

'I'm fine.'

'Janet spoke to me,' Ingrid said. 'I trust her. She said you definitely need help. I'll take you to the appointment.'

It wasn't a question.

The phone rang. Ingrid lifted her knitting off her lap and placed it on the table next to her, then got out of her seat and picked up the receiver.

'Ingrid speaking.'

Finn watched her face as she listened down the line. After a couple of moments she held the receiver out to him.

'It's the police, they want to talk to you.'

Finn took it from her. She went into the kitchen and Finn heard the kettle going.

'Mr Sullivan?'

'Yes.'

'DI Linklater here. We'd like you to come to the station tomorrow morning for a chat.'

'Am I under arrest?'

'No, we just want to talk about a few things.'

'Like what?'

'Some new information has come to light.'

'You're not going to tell me?'

'It's better if we discuss it tomorrow.'

'What if I say no?'

'We'll arrest you and interview you formally. Shall we say nine o'clock? No point putting it off.'

Finn looked at Sky News. They were back with the first woman at the airfield, talking to some expert, the two of them gesticulating, something technical about flight trajectories. The expert had his hand pointing towards earth like an arrow.

'I'll see you tomorrow,' Finn said.

25

The police station was a brick of a thing with tiny windows, squatting next to the Peedie Sea, a bleak stretch of pond flanked by scrubby grass in the middle of Kirkwall. The pond was separated from the harbour and marina by a thin causeway, which also served as the main northwest road out of town. The surface of the Peedie Sea was ruffled by constant wind, the sun throwing strands out from behind broken clouds fizzing across the sky.

'Are you ready?' Ingrid said.

She'd driven him despite his protestations that he could manage fine. He hadn't seen Maddie this morning, couldn't think of an excuse to get away, Ingrid watching him over breakfast. He didn't have much appetite, the morphine for his rib taking the edge off and fuzzing his head. At least that helped him to stay calm over this.

He edged out of the car, his body aching all over despite the painkillers.

Ingrid got out too.

'You can stay here,' Finn said.

'I'm coming in.'

Finn breathed out and stretched but didn't speak.

They went to reception and were told to wait by a busty middle-aged woman who threw Ingrid a look of sympathy. Finn wondered what Maddie was doing right now. He'd texted her when he woke up saying he would pop over, then again an hour later when it was clear he wouldn't be able to. She was flirty, saying she was thinking about him, needed to see him. He thought about her body on top of his, the slight ripples across her belly from the movement, the feeling of him being inside her.

The receptionist got a call.

'You can go through now,' she said, buzzing the security door.

They both got up.

'Just the boy, Ingrid,' the woman said, apology in her voice.

'Come on, Anita.'

The woman held up the phone receiver and shrugged. 'Orders from above.'

Ingrid put a hand on Finn's arm. 'Are you sure you don't need a solicitor?'

'It's just a chat, no need to worry.'

'I'll wait in the car.'

He pushed at the door, keen to get away from the look on her face, disappointment that she couldn't hide. He'd let her down. He was the only family she had left and he was dragging her into the dirt, so soon after what happened with Sally, bringing shame on them both. It was worse for her, of course. He could eventually leave the islands, but Ingrid was Orcadian through and through, this would haunt her until she died.

Linklater met him through the door. She looked fresh-faced and bright-eyed, like she'd had a better night's sleep than Finn.

'Through here,' she said.

It was like another waiting room, three plastic chairs and a low, round coffee table. Blank grey walls, cheap ceiling tiles, square window looking over the Peedie Sea.

'So what's this about?' Finn said.

Linklater held up her phone with the recording app. 'You mind?'

'I've seen the TV shows, don't you have an old cassette thing that beeps? And doesn't there have to be two of you?'

Linklater smiled. 'That's for admissible evidence, formal interviews. I told you, this is just to keep me straight.'

Finn nodded.

She switched the app on, placed the phone on the table between them, then smoothed down her trousers, her hands resting on her knees. 'We've had some developments, as I mentioned last night.'

'Have you found Maddie?'

Linklater gave him a look. 'We haven't, but we will.'

'Do you think she's still alive?'

'Oh, yes.'

'What makes you so sure?'

'If she died in the crash we would've found her body by now.'

'Maybe she was injured, confused, maybe she walked off and died further away.'

'You know the conditions that night,' Linklater said. 'She couldn't have gone far, not without help.'

This was directed at Finn.

'I wouldn't know about that,' he said. 'I was in hospital.'

'Of course.' Linklater shifted her weight in the chair. 'So we spoke to Claire Buchan yesterday.'

'Who?'

'You don't know her?'

'No.'

'Madeleine's best friend. We asked if she'd heard from Madeleine since the crash, and she said no. We also told her about Kevin Pierce's death. Naturally she was shocked.'

'What's this got to do with me?'

Linklater stared at him. 'I'm getting to that. She was shocked, said she couldn't imagine Madeleine doing such a thing. But she did hint that things had been difficult between Kevin and Madeleine for a while. Apparently, he was a bully.'

'So you think Maddie did it?'

'We're just gathering information, collecting evidence. That's what we do.'

'I still don't know why you dragged me in for this.'

Linklater smiled. 'The thing is, we also had a wee chat with some of Claire's neighbours. She lives in Stromness, in Hellihole Road. Do you know it?'

Finn shook his head.

'One of her neighbours had something interesting to say. Can you think what it might be?'

'Surprise me.'

'Someone fitting your description was round there yesterday, chatting to Mrs Buchan at her front door. They seemed to be having an argument. The person only left when Claire's husband turned up and warned him off.'

Finn breathed out through his nose and laid his hands out in front of him.

'OK, I was there. I know how it looks but I went to see her for the same reason you did, to find out if she'd heard from Maddie.'

Linklater shook her head. 'How did you know about her? How did you know Claire was Madeleine's best friend?'

'It's not hard to find stuff out. You told me Maddie lived in Stromness so I went there. I walked into the hotel bar and asked, the same in the harbour cafe. They were all talking about the crash and Maddie. Some old dear told me about Claire, where she lived. I went and asked the same thing you did. That's it.'

'That's ludicrous.'

'It's what happened.'

'You know we'll check your story.'

'Go ahead.'

'You don't want to change it?'

Finn shook his head.

'What exactly did you and Mrs Buchan say to each other?'

'I asked if she'd heard from Maddie since the crash.'

'Did you mention Kevin Pierce?'

Finn thought about that. 'No.'

'You don't sound too sure.'

'I'm sure.'

'And what did you say to Lenny?'

'Who's Lenny?'

'The husband.'

'Nothing. He just told me to leave.'

'So you left.'

'Yeah.'

Linklater sat back in her chair. 'I hope you realise what an almighty mess you're in.'

'OK, I admit going round there was stupid,' Finn said. 'But it was an innocent mistake.'

'We'll check your story and when it doesn't pan out you're going to have a lot more explaining to do. Just to warn you.

And between now and the next time we meet, I'd advise you to stay at home, OK?'

'Sure.'

'Leave the police work to us,' Linklater said. 'And maybe spend some time finding a solicitor. You're going to need one.'

'Are we finished?'

Linklater sighed. 'No. We've spoken to Sean Bayliss.'

'He's out of his coma?'

'We got his account of events on the plane. He admits fighting with you, but claims he only retaliated after you hit him first.'

Finn shifted in his seat. 'I told you, that's not how it was. He was harassing Maddie, I was trying to help.'

'By starting a fight on an aeroplane.'

'By trying to get him away from her.'

'Charlotte Woodside confirms Mr Bayliss's version of events.'

'She didn't see the whole thing, she was busy up front.'

'It's very likely you'll be charged with assault and causing a disruption on an aircraft to the risk of fellow passengers.'

'That's ridiculous.'

'Count yourself lucky, it could be seven counts of culpable manslaughter.'

'I was trying to help.'

Linklater narrowed her eyes. 'Well, without Madeleine's version of events, we can only go with what we have. If we find her alive, maybe she can back up your story. But as it is . . .'

She let that hang between them.

Finn's chest rose and fell, his lungs like rocks. He thought about the blood he'd coughed up last night. 'Are we finished?'

Linklater reached over and switched the recording app off. 'For now. But you'll be hearing from me again.'

Finn stood up and felt light-headed. He opened the door.

'Finn?' Linklater said, concerned. 'I don't know what kind of hold she has over you, but I hope she's worth it.'

26

Finn was surprised there were no police or hospital security. It had taken him less than ten minutes to walk up the hill from the police station to the Balfour. When he left the station, Ingrid was in the Skoda with her head in a paperback and he made a decision, turned left round the side of the building, left again along the bank of the Peedie Sea where she couldn't see him. He came out at the supermarket car park and followed the road round, collar turned up partly against the wind, partly to hide his face.

And now here he was next to Sean Bayliss's bed. He'd just walked into the hospital and checked the signs, looked in every ward as if he knew what he was doing, a confident stride covering the shakiness in his legs. It felt like he was trespassing somehow. Was there a law against going to see someone in hospital? Maybe there was, if you were about to be charged with assault against them.

He found Sean after ten minutes of sticking his head in each door as he went past. No stern matron warning him off, just overworked nurses scurrying about trying to hold the place together.

Sean looked contented. He was sleeping, propped up on pillows, a clean white bandage around one ear and the side of his head. Finn tried to remember what he looked like in the wreckage but all he could picture was the other guy on the floor with the metal sticking out from his spine. One of Sean's friends. Three of his best friends dead, how did that feel? Or maybe they weren't his friends at all, maybe just colleagues, bonding over a trip home. Perhaps they all hated Sean, the show-off of the group, the macho alpha male, the one who would go up to women and harass them with impunity. Or maybe they loved him for that, for daring to do what they couldn't, for entertaining them with his sexist shit.

Finn stood over Sean, watched his chest rise and fall.

'Hey,' he said.

Sean snuffled and turned his head, shifted under the sheets a little.

'Hey,' Finn said, louder this time.

Sean's eyes fluttered open, unfocused for a moment, then he recognised Finn. He pushed himself up on his elbows, away from Finn, who was so close to the bed he was touching the sheet wrapped around the side of the mattress, his leg pressing against the metal support underneath.

'What the hell do you want?' Sean said.

'Just to talk.'

'I've got nothing to say to you.'

'You had plenty to say about me to the police.'

Sean looked past Finn at the entrance to the ward. There were three other beds in the room, none of them occupied though two had signs of patients, flowers on one bedside, the remains of a meal on a tray at the other.

'I have a button,' Sean said, lifting a small box from the side of the covers. 'If I press it, a nurse comes running.'

'Go ahead,' Finn said. 'I don't give a shit.'

Sean hesitated. 'I just told the cops what I remembered.'

Finn narrowed his eyes. 'You seemed to miss out the bit where you assaulted Maddie.'

'I never touched that stupid cow,' Sean said. 'I was just talking to her.'

Finn looked around. 'There's no need to lie when it's just the two of us. I know what happened. I saw you. You had hold of her arm.'

'So what? She wanted me to touch her, she was flirting.'

'It wasn't flirting and you know it.'

'Some women like a bit of rough, what can I say?'

Finn pictured himself burying his fist into the guy's guts, scraping the metal splint on his hand down Sean's face. He stood there at the side of the bed squeezing his good fist.

'You're a fucking arsehole,' he said.

Sean smiled. 'I'm the fucking arsehole who's going to put you in prison.'

Finn shook his head. 'I'm not the one going to prison, you are.'

The smile faded from Sean's face. 'It's you and that psycho bitch that caused all this.' He lifted a hand to the bandages at his head. 'Three of my mates are dead and I was in a coma all because you and that cow couldn't take a joke. I was only messing with the pair of you, for fuck's sake. But you got your macho bollocks on and had to defend her honour or whatever. Idiot.'

'People like you can't be allowed to get away with how you behave.'

'Who do you think you are, telling me what I can't do?' Sean said, voice raised. 'You acted like a baby and got everyone on that plane killed. You don't get to tell me anything.'

'I didn't kill anyone.' Finn's voice was raised as well now, tinny in his ears.

'I'm going to make sure you pay for what you did to my mates.'

Finn grabbed Sean's shoulder tight and shook him. 'I didn't kill anyone.'

Sean pushed his hand away and backhanded Finn across the cheek, raising blood to the surface, tears to his eyes. Finn grabbed Sean's wrist and pushed, then raised his hand to hit him.

'What the hell is going on here?'

A female voice behind him. Finn dropped his hands to his sides as Sean beamed.

'It's OK, nurse, he's just leaving.'

Finn didn't turn, kept staring at Sean, looking for something in his eyes.

'Are you the other man from the plane?' the nurse said.

Finn turned. She was forty and slim, pretty eyes and flat shoes.

'That's him,' Sean said.

'You can't be in here,' the nurse said. 'You have to leave immediately.'

'That's what I was telling him,' Sean said.

Finn was unable to speak. The nurse took him by the elbow and guided him towards the door.

'I can't imagine what you think you're doing here,' she said.

'Threatening me, that's what he's doing,' Sean shouted after them.

Finn could hear the laughter in Sean's voice, goading him.

The nurse got him out of the ward and stopped at the first set of doors. She turned to him. 'Why did you come here?'

Finn shook his head and pushed through the doors.

27

Cromwell Road was on a rise to the northeast of Kirkwall, views over the marina and beyond that to the harbour. A ferry chugged out into the choppy surface of the sea, heading north to one of the smaller islands, churning water and diving terns in its wake. The sun was low in the sky, a smattering of high clouds throwing drizzle into the air, a faint whisper of a rainbow over the bay. Finn turned to look at the house. Standard rough-cladding Orkney place, with blue trim around the doors and windows to try to make it stand out. He checked the number against the information on his phone, walked up the short path and rang the doorbell, stepping back to look at the windows.

A short, solid man in his fifties opened the door. Wavy white hair swept back, blood colouring his cheeks and nose. A drinker. He wore paint-spattered overalls and a checked shirt underneath.

'Is Charlotte home?' Finn said.

The man frowned. 'Who's asking?'

'I'm a friend of hers.'

'No, you're not.' The man squinted into the light of the huge sky behind Finn, then his eyes widened. 'You're the laddie from the plane.'

'Is she here?'

'You stay away from my Charlotte. You've done enough damage.'

Finn closed his eyes and pinched the bridge of his nose.

'It was an accident,' he said. 'Fog and turbulence. I had nothing to do with it.'

The man stepped forward and pulled the door behind him. 'Do you have any idea what our girl has been through?'

Finn wanted to say something but he didn't.

'She's been crying her eyes out ever since,' the man continued. 'Hasn't left the house. God knows if she'll be able to go back to work.'

'I just need to speak to her.'

The man shook his head. 'No chance. You've got to be kidding.'

'Dad?'

Finn recognised her voice. The door opened and the man looked flustered for a moment, reached for the door handle too late.

'Nothing to worry about, love,' he said. 'He's leaving.'

She wore a baggy Aberdeen Uni hoodie and black leggings. Her hair was up in a loose bun and her hands were thrust into the pouch pocket of the hoodie. Her features seemed more raw than on the plane, but her eyes were calm and she didn't show surprise at the sight of Finn on her front step.

'It's OK, Dad,' she said, widening the door.

'No it bloody isn't,' her dad said.

She was taller than him by a few inches and had a natural authority. She didn't look like someone suffering from shock, but then what did Finn know about that? She put a hand on her dad's shoulder and smiled.

'Put the kettle on,' she said. 'I'll speak to him.'

Her dad looked from her to Finn then back. 'It's not a good idea.'

She rubbed his shoulder and moved aside to let him go back in. 'Tea. Go. I'll be done in two minutes.'

Her dad hesitated then left, looking defeated by his inability to protect his daughter.

Charlotte pressed her mouth into a line and turned to Finn.

'How are you?' she said.

He wasn't expecting that. He was expecting to be asked what he was doing here, how dare he come.

'OK, considering. How are you?'

She pulled a hand from her pocket and pushed a tissue against her nose as she sniffed. She shook her head a little, as if to herself.

'Sometimes I think I'm fine, but then I picture it all over again. I saw that English couple, you know. I was right there. I don't think I'll ever get that out of my mind.'

'I'm sorry.'

'I tried to go out for a walk earlier. Just along the road, get some air. Everything seemed dialled down, you know? Like the cars weren't really cars, the houses were only shadows of houses. It's hard to explain. Do you understand?'

'I think so,' Finn said.

'But then other times it's the opposite,' Charlotte said. 'The world is just too much in your face. Putting clothes on, going to the toilet, it's all just too bright and difficult.' She held out her hand, palm up, a red welt along the outer edge. 'I burnt myself on the toaster this morning. Just had my hand against it. Didn't realise until it was already blistered. What's wrong with me?'

'You've been through a lot.'

She looked him in the eye. She seemed kinder without her glasses on. Finn wondered if her glasses had survived the crash.

'What about you?' she said. 'It can't be easy. Everyone is blaming you.'

Finn scratched at the back of his head but didn't speak.

'You and the woman,' Charlotte said.

'What about you? Do you blame me?'

Charlotte put her hands into her pockets and looked at her feet. 'I don't think it was anyone's fault really.'

'But you spoke to the police. Told them I hit that guy.'

'I told them what I remembered. I couldn't lie.'

'He was being an arsehole to Maddie.'

Charlotte nodded. 'I know. I told the police that too. But I saw you hit him. I had to tell them. You understand?'

Finn looked at her and felt like crying.

'Sure.'

There was silence. Finn could sense her dad lingering in the hallway behind the door. He heard the noise of the kettle in the kitchen.

'Why did you come here?' Charlotte said eventually.

'I wanted to see if you were OK,' Finn said, then hesitated. 'No, that's not true. When I was walking here I wanted to speak to you, get you to change what you said to the police. But I don't now, I'm just glad you're all right.'

Charlotte took the tissue out again, held it to her nose.

'There's a memorial later,' she said. 'For the others.'

Finn nodded. 'Are you going?'

'I can't decide. Are you?'

'I feel like I should, but it's hard.'

'I'm the same, I don't know if I can handle it.'

Finn smiled. 'Well, if I go, I hope I see you there.'

Charlotte nodded and Finn made to leave. He wanted to touch her but he didn't.

'Take care of yourself,' Charlotte said, closing the door.

'Same to you.'

28

Finn looked at the card in his hand. This was the right address for the counsellor but the door said *The Centre for Nordic Studies*, a silhouette of a longship stencilled on the glass and a spread of Scandinavian flags in the window.

He looked around Kiln Corner then pushed open the door.

A young woman with blonde highlights and a thick jumper sat at a reception desk, the walls behind her covered in maps and posters of Vikings.

'I'm looking for Janet Jott,' Finn said.

The woman looked up from her computer and pointed. 'Down the hall, last on the right.'

Finn walked past a rack of leaflets advertising summer courses in island studies and Viking culture. The door said *Dr Janet Jott*. He knocked.

'Come in.'

It wasn't much more than a supply cupboard and the door opened inwards, nearly touched her desk on its sweep. There were shelves of textbooks along one wall, a view out the window of a lock-up garage and a large flag on the other wall. It was one-third red and two-thirds navy blue, a circle of reversed colours overlapping the two, green and yellow stripes down the divide.

'Cool flag,' Finn said.

'The Sami people,' Janet said. 'Indigenous across the Finnish and Russian Arctic. The circle represents the sun and the moon. They call themselves the children of the sun.'

Finn gauged the room and her. She seemed in her element surrounded by academia. 'So counselling isn't a full-time gig?'

'Very few things are these days,' Janet said, gesturing. 'Take a seat.'

Finn stalled for a moment, staring at the seat, then sat down. 'I don't know why I'm here.'

'Because we had an appointment.'

'I was in the neighbourhood, otherwise I wouldn't have bothered. I was visiting the police again.'

'About the accident?'

'Partly.'

'It can't be easy for you.'

Finn laughed. 'You think?'

'It's perfectly normal to be defensive. Textbook response, in fact.'

'Aren't you supposed to be more touchy-feely?'

Janet closed the laptop on her desk and focused on him. 'I've found over the years that a more direct approach tends to work better around here. Orcadians don't appreciate pussyfooting around.'

Finn waved his hand around the room. 'So tell me how all this works. You're a professor by day, a counsellor by night?'

'I'm only a doctor, not a professor,' Janet said. 'It's simple really, two part-time jobs make one modest living. Very different experiences, but equally rewarding. I get to help people in different ways.'

Finn held up the card she'd given him at the hospital. 'How does this work?' He looked around the tiny room. 'You don't have space for a psychiatrist's sofa.'

'Shrinks haven't used leather sofas in fifty years, it's a movie cliché. We just sit and chat.'

'For how long?'

'As long as you like.'

'What if I want to leave?'

Janet pointed at the door. 'Close it on the way out.'

Finn smiled. 'How do you know Ingrid?'

'We met at night school.'

'Night school?'

Janet nodded. 'There was no university or college on Orkney back then. I'm talking mid-seventies. If you wanted education after school you left the islands or went to night classes.'

'And you didn't fancy leaving?'

'I couldn't really. My folks needed me on the farm, couldn't manage without me. Ingrid was in the same boat, that's how we came to be friends.'

'What did you study?'

Janet pointed at the flag. 'Viking culture and indigenous people of the North. That sort of stuff. There wasn't much in the way of courses in all that in those days, it was frowned upon. Our culture wasn't thought worthy of study. Looking back on it, that's pretty disgraceful. But we got lucky with a local guy who was a self-taught expert.'

'And Ingrid did the same courses?'

Janet nodded. 'I suppose it started us on the road to where we are today.'

'But all Gran does is show tourists round the Tomb of the Eagles.'

Janet shrugged. 'It's a matter of self-respect and pride. When we grew up, being Orcadian was nothing to shout about, local culture was put down or ignored. Now the opposite is true.' She pointed to a framed diploma on the wall. 'I'm a doctor in Nordic studies, internationally respected expert on the Sami.' Her voice played with the words 'internationally respected' to debunk them a little, but she was still proud.

'And a trauma counsellor,' Finn said.

'Indeed.'

'How did you get into that?'

Janet's face fell for a moment and she swallowed.

'I had trauma of my own,' she said softly. 'That's how most people get into it.'

Finn looked at her. 'You don't have to tell me.'

'It's fine. When I was ten, my mother left me in the car with my little sister while she went to get her messages from the shops. I was playing with the handbrake and I took it off. The car began rolling and I couldn't stop it. There were no seatbelts in those days. I only had a few bruises but Caitlin broke her neck.'

'Christ,' Finn said.

Janet glanced at him then out the window. 'It was a long time ago.'

'Still.'

'I held that with me, took years to get over it. Of course, you never really do, something like that. We never had any therapy or counselling up here in those days, social services didn't really know how to cope. Neither did my folks.'

'I can't imagine,' Finn said.

'I think you can, after what happened the other night. Anyway, that's why I do this.'

'Is that all there is to it?' Finn said. 'Experiencing the shitness of life?'

Janet shrugged. 'Do you believe in God?'

'No.'

'Me neither. Christians like to say that God gets you through hardships, that without him you feel alone and helpless. But that's bullshit, pardon my language.'

Finn laughed.

'I've always found the opposite,' Janet said. 'The fact that there isn't any great master plan makes it easier to take all the crap that life throws at you. Once you realise it's all random and doesn't matter in the scheme of things, it's much easier to get distance from the awful things that happen to everyone all the time.'

'This is some pep talk,' Finn said.

'It is what it is.' Janet got up from behind her desk and came round to Finn's side, perched on a corner. 'I don't pretend to have answers and to do so would be dishonest and disrespectful. How do you feel about the accident?'

Finn stared at the lines around her eyes, the grey in her hair, the traces of a life lived. 'Kind of numb.'

Janet nodded. 'It's early days, that's to be expected. It's a long road, Finn. That's not the kind of advice you young people want to hear, but it's true. It can take months or years before you come to some arrangement in your mind with what's happened. Sometimes you never do. It certainly never completely disappears. I know that with Caitlin.'

'This really isn't pick-me-up banter.'

'If you want that, go find a cheerleader or a life coach. That's not what I do.'

Finn looked out the window. The faint sound of church bells floated into the office in between the whipping of the wind.

'I don't know anything about those people,' he said.

'The ones on the plane?'

Finn nodded. 'Seven dead.'

'And the girl still missing.'

Finn looked Janet in the eye. 'Yeah.'

'Still no word on her from the police?'

'Nothing new.'

'I hope she turns up. It must be hard for her, wherever she is.'

Finn held his hands out. 'Seven people dead because of me, that's seven times what you managed with your sister.'

'You didn't kill those people.'

'Didn't I?'

'No, and I think you know it.'

'You have more faith in me than I have in myself.'

Janet shook her head. 'No, I don't. You just don't know yourself very well at the moment. You're capable of extraordinary things, the same as everyone else.'

'I wish I believed that.'

The church bells were louder now, more insistent.

'You will,' Janet said.

Finn stood up and went to the window. He felt her eyes on him. 'So what do I do now?'

'That's up to you.'

'Isn't there a twelve-point plan or something?'

'There's no single way of dealing with what you've been through.'

'Some therapist you are.'

'I'm a counsellor.'

'Some counsellor, then.'

'You want me to wave a magic wand?' Janet mimicked a fairy godmother, sweeping her hand in front of her. 'Whoosh! There, all better now.'

Finn gave her a sideways look. 'Does this method work with other trauma victims?'

'It's a starting point.'

Something was nagging at Finn. 'Why are they ringing the cathedral bells at this time of day?'

'I presumed you knew.'

Finn frowned for a second then it came to him. 'The memorial service.'

Janet nodded.

'The police told me not to go,' Finn said.

'That's good advice, I suppose.'

'You don't sound convinced.'

'Some of the relatives will be feeling very angry. If you show up, you could be a focus for that.'

'So I shouldn't go?'

'I didn't say that. It's up to you.'

'If I don't go it looks like I don't care. I want to show that it hurts me too, everything that's happened. I want to show respect for those people.'

There was just the tumble of bells falling through the wind outside.

Finn looked back out the window. 'I didn't kill them. I didn't do anything wrong. I want to go and pay my respects.'

'OK.'

Finn looked at Janet and took a deep breath. 'Will you come with me?'

She replied without missing a beat.

'Sure.'

29

Broad Street in front of St Magnus Cathedral was rammed. Several television broadcast vans were parked outside the medieval sandstone building. The babble of voices and the bright lights were dizzying. The road was full of people, the whole of Orkney must be out. There was an air of sombre propriety among the older ones, but kids were mucking around too, teenagers acting cool, mums trying to control toddlers, occasionally a face that Finn recognised from visiting the islands over the years.

His phone pinged in his pocket. A message from Ingrid wondering where he was. In fact, three messages from her in the hours since he avoided her outside the police station. In amongst them was a message from Amy saying she was on her way north. He typed a reply to Ingrid:

Heading to memorial.

Then he put his phone away and looked around. Crowds were backed all the way along Albert Street and West Castle Street, hundreds of people out to show support.

His phone pinged again.

Palace Road side entrance. Meet you there.

He touched Janet's arm.

'Round the back,' he said.

He led her up Laing Street on to School Place then over the low wall at the back of the cathedral. They walked through the gravestones to the southern entrance, the side they used when the winds were too high to leave the front doors open.

Some people on Palace Road watched them as they stepped through the graveyard. Reporters and journalists round the front couldn't see them from here. Finn didn't know if that was good or bad. Wasn't part of this to show that he cared? Shouldn't he be seen going in? But it was more important just to be there, to show the dead people's families that he cared, and to hell with the rest of the world.

He pulled open the side door and let his eyes adjust to the gloom. Before he could put a foot inside, Linklater was in front of him.

'I told you not to come,' she said.

Finn looked beyond her at the congregation. The main body of the cathedral was already packed. Subdued organ music and the odd scuffing of chair legs against the flagstone floor reverberated around the cavernous ceiling.

'I had to,' Finn said.

'Go home.'

'I'll vouch for him,' Janet said. She gave him a smile that was supposed to be reassuring.

Linklater shook her head. 'I'm sorry, Janet, it's not a good idea.'

'You haven't charged him with anything yet,' Janet said. 'He's free to do what he likes.'

Linklater stepped on to the threshold and pulled the heavy door behind her.

'This doesn't concern you, Janet.'

'Perhaps not professionally but I'm not here in that capacity.'

'Why are you here?' Linklater said. 'Have you any idea what he's mixed up in?'

'I have some notion.'

Linklater looked at Finn. 'I bet you haven't told her the whole story.'

Janet frowned. 'It doesn't matter what he's told me. I'm trying to help.'

'Me too.' It was a new voice behind Finn. Ingrid.

Linklater looked at her. 'Please tell me you're here to take him home.'

Ingrid was out of breath. 'That's entirely up to him.'

'No, it's up to me,' Linklater said, 'and I'm telling you to take him home.'

'If I don't?'

Linklater sighed. 'Do you really want to get into this? There are people in there who want him strung up. Literally. I just want this thing to go off without any more distress for anyone.'

Ingrid stepped forward and laid a hand on the stonework. Finn imagined a Viking lord doing the same thing eight hundred years ago. She gave him a serious look. 'Do you want to go through with this?'

'Yes.' His voice was squeaky, pathetic.

Ingrid turned to Linklater. 'I promise I'll look after him. We'll stay out of the way, up the back. And we'll leave before the end, no lingering. No one will even know we're there.'

Another voice from behind the half-closed door.

'Boss?'

Linklater did an eye-roll and pushed the door open. A tall, broad kid in uniform with square shoulders and a fat face looked nervous.

'What is it?' she said.

'There's a disturbance at the front door,' he said, apologetic.

'What kind of disturbance?'

'Involving one of the film crews and a few locals.'

'So deal with it, that's what you're paid for.'

'Someone has asked for you specifically.'

'Who?'

'I don't know.'

'You didn't ask their name?'

The kid's face went red. 'No.'

'Jesus.' Linklater turned to Ingrid and threw a thumb in Finn's direction. 'OK, you can bring him in, but do exactly as you promised.'

'I will,' Ingrid said.

'Don't make me regret this,' Linklater said, then disappeared into the gloom, following the young officer to the front door.

Ingrid, Finn and Janet slipped inside and Finn heard the door click behind him.

The women walked him along the south wall away from the front door, hugging the shadows as they passed the rows of seats to their left. Finn felt like he was being escorted out of a club by bouncers at closing time. He glanced at the folk sitting down, hoping to catch a glimpse of something meaningful, a tear-stained cheek being dabbed, a comforting arm around a shoulder.

They continued up the nave, past the transepts and into the

chapel, effectively backstage. They walked past the remains of St Magnus then stopped at the corner amongst the memorials. Finn touched the reclining statue of Arctic explorer John Rae and stared at the wall plaques for famous literary men. George Mackay Brown, Edwin Muir and Eric Linklater. He wondered how Morna Linklater was related. He presumed she was, everyone here was, and the Linklaters were one of the big families. He looked down the kirk at the front doors, but couldn't make out what was happening there.

Janet touched his shoulder and handed him a folded sheet of A5. The order of service. 'Picked it up down there.'

Ingrid looked at them, then at the raised dais the organ sat on. She frowned. 'We shouldn't be here. This was a bad idea.'

Finn took the order of service and looked at it. Hymns and prayers, a poetry reading, something by Mackay Brown that he recognised the title of. He flipped the sheet over and there was the information he wanted.

John Tolbert
Mary Tolbert
Evan Reilly
Brian Dean
Graham Wallace
Stephen McDonald
Derek Drennan

John and Mary must be the Yorkshire couple. He wondered if they had kids, if they were here now, had flown up as soon as they could after a terrible phone call or maybe they saw it on the news first. Had it sunk in yet, as they sat in this old building on a windswept island, that they were never going to see their parents again?

Which one was the co-pilot, the one who restrained Sean? What about his family? Maybe a wife and two young kids with no dad any more. Of the other names, one was the pilot, the other three were Sean's workmates. All returning home from work at the oil terminal, looking forward to Christmas, turkey and trimmings, nipping off to the pub if they could, making the most of their time before they had to slog northwards again to earn a wage.

The ripples spreading out were dreadful. Finn imagined an earthquake under his feet, shaking the cathedral's foundations, the sandstone collapsing into nothing, great slabs cascading down on their heads, a shockwave spreading across the islands, wiping out buildings and people like a nuclear blast, ripping skin from bone, tearing at plants and animals, scorching the grass and bracken and heather until there was nothing but black, dead rock for hundreds of miles.

The order of service trembled in his hand. He stared at the names as Ingrid touched his back.

'Are you all right?'

He felt as if his legs would buckle and put out a hand to steady himself. The stone wall was cold and he rubbed a finger up and down, watching as tiny grains of sand fell to the floor. He pictured a Stone Age family going about the business of staying alive down at the South Ronaldsay cliffs, starting a fire, cooking fish, mending clothing, huddled in the warmth of their homestead, happy to be thriving. Now just a row of skulls.

He thought about Maddie in the Lewis house, pulling her panties back on as she got out of bed, the smell of sex in the air. He thought of Kevin screwing Claire, Maddie walking in. He pictured Kevin with a look of surprise on his face, a knife hanging out of his gut, blood sprayed over his chest, the mess of it slithering around him as he lay there trying to breathe.

Finn felt pain in his chest and coughed. Something came into his mouth, metallic, and he knew it was blood. He swallowed it back down, felt it slide into his gut. He choked a little, coughed again, seemed unable to stop. He leaned against the wall, the order of service still in his hand, crumpled up against the stonework.

Eventually he got control of his lungs and straightened up.

'I've changed my mind,' he said. 'We should go.'

Just then the organ music swelled, sombre minor chord changes, tones bouncing around the chapel and back down the nave, sweeping over the mourners.

Finn breathed in, chest tight.

'Come on,' Janet said, guiding him. Ingrid flanked him on the other side. They stayed close to the wall, the light from the stained glass coming in over their heads. They passed a couple of headstones set into the wall, comical depictions of skeletons, skulls and crossbones, the grim reaper with a scythe in one hand and an hourglass in the other.

On the walk back to the exit they were facing the congregation. This time Finn kept his eyes to the wall, the piece of paper still clutched in his hand.

'Hey.' A woman's voice from the seats.

'Keep walking,' Ingrid said under her breath.

'Hey.'

The organ music blossomed then drained. It felt like a living thing, as if the cathedral was a giant lung and the music was the breath sweeping in and out of it.

Finn looked up. A woman in a black dress was excusing herself from her row, walking towards him.

He stopped.

'Come on,' Janet said, pulling him.

'No.' Finn straightened up to face the woman. This was what he was here for, this was what he deserved.

The woman was short and thin, raven hair in a high ponytail. She was in a black dress and heels, a tissue crumpled in one fist. Her mouth was turned down, her eyes red, and he could sense anger radiating off her.

'You're the guy from the plane,' she said in a soft Glasgow accent.

Everyone in the place was watching. The organ music thrummed in Finn's ears. Ingrid stepped close to him. He wanted to push her away. This wasn't something he needed protection from, quite the opposite.

He nodded.

'Because of you, my husband and his friends are dead.'

Finn wondered which one was her husband. One of the oil workers, but which? The guy with the spike through his back? He wanted to uncrumple the order of service, hold it out to her and ask.

'I'm sorry,' he said.

The woman was crying, shaking. 'You bastard.'

'It wasn't my fault.'

'You started a fight,' she said. 'The plane turned round.'

'It wasn't like that,' Finn said. 'There was fog.'

'Shut up,' the woman said. 'Don't speak to me. You don't get to speak.'

He offered himself up to it, hands by his sides, leaving himself open. He waited for the hit and blinked heavily. She threw her weight into a punch, a jab to his chest that doubled him over. He stumbled forward and she lifted her foot and kicked her heel into his groin. He curled up and collapsed, felt her sharp toe as she jammed it into his back, his kidneys aching.

'You bastard,' she said, kicking and kicking.

He accepted it, embraced it. Each blow was deserved, pain sweeping over him like a blanket as he gave up control of himself.

But it didn't last. He heard Ingrid and Janet intervene, then a male voice, older, calming, whispering to the woman as she sobbed and sniffed and made noises more like an animal than a person.

The music swirled around and through him, and he imagined that his curled-up body was a blood clot waiting to be expelled from this enormous lung, an infection ready to spread through the islands.

30

The Highland Park was a shot to his brain. He felt the burn rising from his gut. He put down the empty whisky glass and picked up the bottle of Dark Island, took several slugs, the gulps hurting his rib.

Ingrid and Janet sat across from him with nips of their own.

Finn took the crumpled order of service out of his pocket and laid it on the table. He carefully smoothed it out, bending the corners back over where they'd creased, until it was as flat as he could get it. He traced his fingers over the list of names as if he was blind and it was written in Braille. He stared at the names and listened to his own breathing then lifted his beer.

'Here's to them.'

'*Slainte*,' Janet said, then sipped.

Ingrid's phone buzzed. 'It's Amy wondering where you are. You're not answering your phone.'

Finn had put it on silent in the cathedral out of respect. As if it was that easy to show respect.

Ingrid began texting and Finn looked round. The Bothy Bar was brown and dingy, framed black-and-white fishing and farming pictures on the wall. A stuffed puffin in one corner, some flotsam from a wreck in another. Half a dozen locals lined the bar but the tables were empty apart from Finn and the women, everyone still at the memorial. It was only a hundred yards down the road, but the pub was hidden in a wee nook between roads, the side door of a hotel that never had any visitors.

Three of the regulars had roll-up fags tucked behind their ears, taking it in turns to nip out and smoke them. One guy with a braided grey beard was talking in a West Country accent about Genesis, how they compared before and after Peter Gabriel, as a tall barmaid with an overbite pretended to listen. All kinds of wreckage washed up in Orkney, attracted by the solitude and space. It was a place to drop out of the world.

Finn took another drink of his dark beer.

'Are you happy now?' Janet said.

Finn turned and saw kindness in her face. 'What?'

'That's what you wanted, wasn't it?' She nodded out the tiny window. 'To be punished.'

Finn shook his head. 'No.'

Ingrid put her phone away. 'You could've fooled me.'

'You don't understand,' Finn said, staring at the order of service.

Ingrid sat forward. 'Oh, that's right, you're the only one suffering. You're the only one going through hell. I'm glad that woman beat you up, you deserve it. You're still alive, you're here, her husband isn't.'

'Because of me.'

'Neither of us is saying that,' Janet said.

'You don't need to.'

Finn raised his head. Janet had taken Ingrid's hand in hers and was squeezing it in reassurance. She didn't take her hand away, kept it there but relaxed her grip. Now they looked like a couple in the first throes of love. They gave each other a glance. Finn raised his eyebrows at Ingrid. She sent him a defiant look and squeezed Janet's hand.

Finn was about to speak when the barmaid came over and picked up his shot glass. She was wearing a Bench hoodie and white jeans. 'You guys interested in food?' she said with a Belfast accent.

Ingrid put a hand up. 'No thanks, love.'

Finn watched as the barmaid went back behind the bar. She spoke under her breath to one of the guys at the gantry. She'd been on a recce mission to check if it was him, the guy off the plane, the one who started the fight. The two of them were pretending not to look over, along with Braided Beard, who'd stopped his monologue about the *Duke* album and was stroking his tobacco pouch on the bar.

The door opened and a young woman came in. With the light behind her, Finn couldn't make out her features, but he recognised the body language straight away.

'Oh, Finn,' Amy said.

He got out of his seat, his back aching, those kicks in the kirk echoing in his muscles as he stiffened up.

'Hey.'

He flinched as she hugged him, grimacing at the pain. She squeezed and held on, not letting go.

'Baby,' she said in his ear. 'I've been so worried.'

Eventually she loosened her grip but still held his arms, rubbing her hands along his biceps. She made a show of checking him out, her eyes darting around his face, body, falling on his splinted hand. She lifted and stroked it.

She was thinner than Maddie, taut skin across pale cheeks, her short black hair in a chopped fringe. She wore her puffy North Face jacket that went to her knees, almost like a sleeping bag.

She put a hand to his face, touched his cheek. He was disgusted with himself. What a bastard. Amy had looked after him since his mum died and this was how he repaid her. He felt dizzy and his body swayed.

'You seem a little out of it,' Amy said.

He stared at her. 'Maybe.'

'Well I'm here to look after you,' she said. 'I won't let you out of my sight.'

She took her jacket off, tight jeans and a loose jumper underneath.

'Can I get anyone a drink?'

Ingrid introduced Janet to Amy, describing her as a friend. Finn thought about that as Amy walked to the bar and he went to the toilets.

As he pissed, a cough rose up in his chest and more stuff came into his mouth. He spat into the urinal, the pink and green of blood and phlegm washed away by his stream of piss. He washed his hands and looked at himself in the mirror for a long time. He remembered doing the same on the plane, his reflection blurry around the edges. Right now he seemed too well defined in the harsh light of the toilet. His eyes looked so tired. He wiped at them and his vision went fuzzy, floaters drifting across his eyeline.

The door opened and Ingrid and Amy bustled in.

'The tabloids are here,' Ingrid said.

Amy nodded. 'Some guy from the *Daily Mail* came in asking questions. Janet is stalling him.'

'What about the rest of the folk at the bar?'

'He hasn't got round to asking them yet, he came to us first,' Ingrid said. 'Janet began talking, I went to the bar pretending to help Amy with the drinks and we came in here.'

'Maybe I should speak to him,' Finn said.

'Absolutely not,' Ingrid said.

'But we're stuck in here,' Finn said. 'And the regulars or the barmaid will say something.'

'Ingrid says we can get out another way,' Amy said. 'Turn right out the door and through the hotel.'

'He'll see us.'

Ingrid shook her head. 'He's facing the other way. Go.'

The three of them went out the door, Ingrid first, then Finn, Amy at the back. Janet was sitting close to the reporter, a balding man squeezed into a shiny suit. Janet didn't look up, just kept talking into a device the reporter held across the table, as Finn and the others slipped along the adjoining corridor and out the Albert Hotel.

Ingrid was still parked at the police station round the corner and they climbed into the car and pulled away. They avoided the centre of town, turning up Junction Road then on to New Scapa Road, Finn's heart pounding. So they were hiding from reporters again. He couldn't run forever.

Ingrid took the main road south and they bumped along, nudging the speed limit.

'Let's just get you home,' she said.

Finn felt Amy's hand touching his neck from the back of the car.

'Everything's going to be all right, babe.'

31

As they came over the rise to Ingrid's cottage, Finn saw a car waiting for them. He recognised it and dug his hand into the back pocket of his jeans, pulled out her card. The girl from the *Orcadian*.

'Christ,' Ingrid said.

'What?' Amy said.

'That's the local reporter. I'm going to give her shit for coming here again.'

Finn peered out the windscreen at the Ford. He could make out Freya's gawky form and black hair. He looked behind them at the Lewis house and the visitor centre, wondered about Maddie inside.

'It's OK, Gran, I'll talk to her.'

'That's not a good idea,' Amy said.

'I know what I'm doing.'

As they pulled up behind her car Freya bundled out, raising her eyebrows in self-deprecation as if to say sorry, me again.

Ingrid cut the engine and got out of the car, Amy and Finn likewise.

Amy was first up to the reporter, sticking her chin out. 'Leave him alone.'

'I don't think we've been introduced,' Freya said, sticking her hand out. 'My name is Freya Magnusson, reporter with the *Orcadian*. And you are?'

'I'm Finn's girlfriend and I'm telling you to piss off.'

Freya flipped open her notebook. 'What's your name?'

Finn put a hand on Amy's arm. 'Let me speak to her.'

The four of them stood there on the headland in the wind, scattered clouds in the sky, the sea below like hammered metal, blinding where the sun caught it. The knuckle of mainland Scotland was clear in this light, and Finn wondered if it was possible to swim that far. Maybe if you trained hard enough and tried it on a calm summer day, but it was suicide otherwise.

He turned to Ingrid. 'You two go inside.'

Amy protested but Finn reassured her and she let Ingrid take her into the cottage.

Freya smiled. 'Girlfriend?'

'What do you want?'

'Have the tabloids caught up with you yet?'

Finn just stood.

Freya nodded. 'They will. Folk here don't talk to strangers much, but they'll find you sooner or later, and they'll be on you like a dog on beetroot.'

'I've asked you already, what do you want?'

She looked at the cottage then turned and stared at the Lewis house, the roof just visible beyond the rise in the road. She turned back to him almost absent-mindedly.

'There have been some developments, as they say.'

'Yeah?'

'Kevin Pierce.'

'What about him?'

'He's turned up dead.'

'Really?'

'I'm not telling you anything you don't already know.'

'Yes, you are.'

Freya tilted her head. 'Either you were involved in it, or the police already told you. Or someone else did.'

Finn kept his eyes on Freya's face, not beyond. He shook his head.

Freya went on. 'Stabbed to death at home, apparently. The police are asking for witnesses to come forward. And more importantly, they're increasing the search for Maddie Pierce, now in connection with her husband's murder.'

Finn rubbed at his finger splint. 'So why are you talking to me?'

She leaned in, lowered her voice. 'Because I know you know something about all this. I know a liar when I see one and you are a terrible liar.'

'Is this how you always go about your work?' Finn said.

Freya snorted with laughter. 'It's usually missing pets and primary-school fairs.'

'Maybe you should stick to that stuff.'

'I'm offering you one last chance,' Freya said. 'Before the *Mail* and all the rest rip you to shreds. Tell your side of the story. If you give me a proper interview, I promise it will be sympathetic.'

'And I should trust a journalist.'

'I'm not like them.' She held out her hand, finger crooked. 'Pinkie promise?'

'Leave me alone.'

Freya put her pen to her notebook.

'Mr Sullivan,' she said in an officious voice. 'Did you have anything to do with the death of Kevin Pierce?'

'Fuck off.'

She made a song and dance about writing 'Fuck off' in the book.

'Were you having an affair with Madeleine Pierce?'

'Fuck off.'

Freya mumbled 'Fuck off' under her breath as she wrote.

'Do you know of Mrs Pierce's whereabouts since the accident?'

Finn sighed. 'I'm going inside to be with my family.'

Freya nodded. 'No comment, good, makes it sound like you know something.'

'Goodbye.'

He began to walk towards the house.

'Goodbye,' Freya shouted after him. 'And good luck.'

Finn went inside and stood with his back to the door. He took a deep breath and closed his eyes. Pictured himself in court, under oath, being asked the same questions. Imagined standing over Kevin Pierce's body with a knife in his hand. Saw himself taking Maddie on the Lewises' bed. Pictured himself in the plane, always in the plane, hitting the ground, his seat thrown backward, losing sight of Maddie, the wing crushing that poor couple who only came here for a winter break, to check out the standing stones, a bit of bird-spotting maybe, some gentle walks along the coastline, their sons and daughters left with no parents, everyone suffering and all of it on his shoulders.

He tried to make his hand into a fist, the unnatural grind of broken bone, the splint not budging. He rubbed at his chest, imagining the blood collecting in his lungs until he drowned in it. His legs went weak and he was about to sink to the floor when he felt a hand on his shoulder.

'You'd better come and see this.'

Ingrid led him through to the living room. The television was on, BBC News. Someone slick and shiny standing outside St Magnus Cathedral, then it cut to a press conference, Linklater in a church hall up on stage, a spread of microphones in front of her. She looked exhausted. Finn wondered if she was sleeping, too much workload, too much stress.

Amy turned to him. 'It's the black box, they've released the audio.'

Maddie's voice burst out, reverberating around the hall, echoing back on itself. Press snappers took pictures of Linklater, the flashes making her look pallid and plastic like a shop dummy.

Maddie's voice cut through the sound of engines straining. She was pleading with the pilot, telling him to turn towards Edinburgh. Saying how she couldn't go back to Orkney, she just couldn't, not after what she'd done, she had to get away, he didn't understand, she was dead if she went back, he might as well slit her throat.

The sound went off.

More flashes from photographers.

Linklater leaned into the microphones. 'So this audio, combined with the discovery of Mr Pierce's body, means we are now looking for Madeleine Pierce in connection with the murder of her husband. We believe that Mrs Pierce is alive and still on the island, and we intend to find her. We are increasing the police search, and no stone on Orkney will be left unturned until we find her. If anyone has any information about her whereabouts, please get in touch immediately.'

She gave out a number and began answering banal questions

from the media, but Finn couldn't hear any more, the sound from the television a million miles away.

He felt Ingrid rub his shoulder and he wanted to shake her off, wanted to run outside and leap off the cliff.

Amy stared at him.

He didn't meet her gaze.

'Finn, who is this woman?' she said.

Finn sensed Ingrid heading for the kitchen, giving them space.

'She's no one.'

'She doesn't seem like no one.'

'I hardly even spoke to her.'

Amy got up and faced him, the television still on in the background. 'I'm not an idiot, I can Google. I've read what the papers are saying.'

'They make up shit all the time, you know that.'

'So you didn't sit with her for hours drinking in the airport lounge?'

'I don't know how long it was.' The sound of his whiny voice was pathetic.

'And you were sitting next to her on the plane.'

'It was nothing.'

'I bet you were chatting her up when you didn't answer my calls.'

'My phone was on silent, I didn't hear it.'

'Were you sitting next to her when I spoke to you?'

'I was in the plane toilet.'

'Were you going to screw her, was that it, join the Mile High Club?'

'My God, the plane crashed . . .'

'I know that,' Amy said, eyes wide. 'I'm not asking about that, I don't give a shit about that, I'm asking about you and her.'

'There was no me and her.'

Finn looked at the television. A picture of Maddie grabbed from her Facebook page showed her in a Mediterranean club somewhere, tight dress, pouting at the camera, a sparkle in her eyes that Finn recognised. Then it cut to another photo of her in a bikini with Jackie O glasses and a sunhat.

'She's beautiful,' Amy said.

'Amy, come on.'

'I can see why you found her attractive.' Amy turned back to Finn. 'The stewardess said you punched this other guy who was chatting her up.'

'He was harassing her,' Finn said. 'Really aggressive.'

'So you were her knight in shining armour?'

Her implication was clear, he'd never punched anyone for her.

'I'm sorry,' Finn said. He couldn't think of anything else to say.

Amy was shaking, he couldn't tell if it was crying or rage. Maybe both.

'I can't even look at you right now,' she said. 'I thought I knew you, Finn.'

'You do, you know me better than anyone.'

*

The rest of the day he expected a knock on the door or the phone to ring, either the police or the press. But there was nothing, which was worse in a way, he wanted the axe to fall. The wait was excruciating. Amy kept her distance and he didn't blame her.

In the living room he picked a battered paperback of Mackay Brown's poetry from Ingrid's shelves and tried to read it. Normally Brown's clarity soothed him, made him think of his mum, but now every line felt ominous. There was a poem actually called 'Thorfinn' that seemed to be about someone drowning. Another line somewhere else jumped out at him: 'But we must die, fast in our web of lust'. Christ.

He felt an overwhelming itch to walk out the door and up to the visitor centre. Or maybe go beyond the Lewis place to the tomb, commune with the dead, hear their stories, listen to their ancient wisdom. Who was he kidding, they were just as stuck in their lives as he was now, searching for the next meal, hoping their nets would be full of fish, checking crops that could be frost-damaged or dried out or flooded. Thousands of years of human life stuck in a rut. Finn was just the end point, the final link in a chain of shit existence.

His phone vibrated in his pocket. He looked up to see if Amy or Ingrid were around. No sign. He went to the bathroom, locked the door, put the toilet lid down and sat on it. Checked the screen. A text from Maddie.

Going mad here, need to see you. Where are you? Mx

He replied:

Me too. It's out about Kevin, black box too. Looks bad.

Can't get away.

His life was over now. His relationship with Amy was over too. What did he imagine, that she would forgive all this? She would find out eventually, and even if she did forgive him, he couldn't live with himself. He had to finish it, he just had to find the right time.

He heard footsteps outside the door and knew it was Amy, she had a lighter step than Ingrid.

His phone vibrated, the buzz echoing round the tiles.

I need you so bad. I want you to touch me. Mx

She was playing him of course, he knew that, but he couldn't help himself.

Later, I promise.

Footsteps receded outside the door. Amy was checking up on him like he was a naughty little kid. But wasn't that exactly how he was behaving?

Can't wait. Mx

He left the bathroom. Amy was waiting for him at the other end of the hall, at the door to the living room. A look on her face. This is it, he thought.

'Something's happened,' she said, glancing back into the room.

'What?'

She waved at the television.

He walked to the doorway and looked. The sound was down on the news, a reporter standing outside the Balfour Hospital. The ticker-tape display along the bottom of the screen said that Sean Bayliss had died from a massive stroke as a result of his head injuries.

'That's not right,' Finn said.

Amy stared at him. Ingrid came through from the kitchen.

'He woke up,' Finn said. 'I spoke to him.'

'You went to see him?' Ingrid said. 'When?'

'He was fine,' Finn said. 'He was awake and talking.'

'When did you see him, Finn?' Amy said.

He shook his head. 'He can't be dead, it doesn't make sense. He just can't be.'

He caught a look between Amy and Ingrid, the two surrogate mothers in his life, a shared worry, a knowing purse of the lips. One of them, he didn't know who, tried to stroke his arm, but he pulled away like the touch was poison.

He stood there looking at the floor, rubbing his hand.

'He can't be dead, he just can't be.'

*

The silence was heavy in the house. He lay in bed in the dark with Amy's head on his chest. Maybe he should do it now, tell her it was over, then at least she would be free of all this, able to escape from whatever he was heading into.

But he didn't, he just held her until her breath slackened and she fell asleep. He waited a long time in that position, staring at the ceiling, the wind birling outside the house, the odd squall of rain slapping the window. He didn't hear anything from Ingrid's room. He slipped his arm out from underneath Amy's embrace and got dressed. At the front door he picked up a torch and left, pulling the door behind him.

32

The three lighthouses on the Pentland Firth blinked out of synch to his right as he walked. He stopped and watched them. The Skerries, Duncansby Head and Stroma, unable to get their act together and flash in unison no matter how long he stared. The moss under his feet was spongy and wet from the rain but the skies were clear now, so many more stars than you saw down south, so much more of the universe on show. Just in case he needed perspective.

He came round the back of the visitor centre. The curtains were pulled shut on the Lewis home, but he went up close and saw the blue flicker of the television screen in the living room, traces of movement filtering through at the edge of the window.

He went to the front door and unlocked it. The sound of the Yale clicking round filled his ears.

He was two steps inside when she emerged from the connecting doorway to the house. He shone the torch in her face and she squinted and held a defensive hand up.

'Sorry,' he said, playing the beam over the floor.

'Thank Christ,' she said when she saw him.

Her voice was ragged, wobbly. Maybe she'd been crying. She'd definitely been drinking. She swayed over and threw her arms around him as he closed the door.

'I've been so worried,' she said. She kissed him on the mouth and he responded without enthusiasm. She pulled away. 'What's the matter?'

'Nothing.'

'Have the police spoken to you again?'

'Should they have?'

'Just wondering.'

'Scared I would give you up?'

She slid a hand down his shirt. 'Of course not.'

He went past her into the front room. The television was on, Sky News. Looked like something about supermarkets at the moment, business news, profits falling.

'I could see the television light from outside,' he said.

'I can't just sit here in the dark.'

He nodded at the television. 'The black box audio is interesting.'

She stepped towards him. 'I know it doesn't sound good but there's nothing I didn't already tell you.'

'The tabloids are after me. I'm amazed they haven't found Ingrid's place yet.'

Maddie looked at the screen, now clips of a football match. 'I saw the reporters at the memorial.'

'I was there.'

'How was it?'

'I got beaten up by someone's widow.'

'Whose?'

Finn dug the order of service out of his pocket and threw it at her. 'Take your pick.'

Maddie scanned the piece of paper, looking at the names, soaking them in just like Finn had done. Perhaps they were the same, him and her.

'My girlfriend's here,' Finn said.

Maddie still had the piece of paper in her hand. 'And?'

'I don't know,' Finn said. 'I don't know anything any more.'

He reached for the order of service and she handed it back. He slumped on the sofa with a heavy sound, sighing like he'd been punched. He wished it was as simple as being punched, then he could just recover and get on with life.

'Everything's closing in,' he said.

'We can handle it.'

He stared at her. 'Is there a "we"?'

She put a hand on his. 'Of course.'

He slipped his hand out from under. 'You have to give yourself up.'

'No.'

He gestured at the television, now showing a politician he vaguely recognised.

'You have to. You didn't kill Kev, right?'

'You know I didn't.'

'Then this is insane.'

She rolled her eyes as if having to explain rocket science to a chimp. 'But I have his money. They won't believe I didn't do it.'

'But forensics . . .'

'They don't give a shit about forensic evidence if they have a murdered husband and a wife with a bag of money yelling at a pilot that she can't go back because of what she's done. Especially if the plane crashes and kills half the people on board.'

'Eight.'

'What?'

'Eight people died. Out of eleven. That's more than half.'

She looked confused. 'You mean seven.'

'Didn't you hear? Sean Bayliss died from his head wounds. A stroke.'

Finn thought of Sally's cold skin under his touch.

'Jesus,' Maddie said.

The smell of alcohol on her was ripe. It made him think of the two of them in the bedroom the night before.

'Is there any of that gin left?' he said, getting up.

'I've moved on to brandy.'

'That'll do.'

He followed her to the drinks cabinet, the television throwing jerky light across the room. It was their story on now, Linklater at the press conference. Maddie glanced at it and kept walking but Finn stopped and stared. The sound was off and the banner across the bottom read 'Murder Hunt in Orkney'.

He took a large tumbler of brandy from her and scooped most of it straight off. Loved the burn. He swallowed the rest of it as she watched him. When he lowered the glass Linklater had gone from the screen, replaced by some footage of the wrecked plane, then the same Facebook picture of Maddie, pouting selfie in a club, shimmering dress, make-up, big hair.

He looked from the screen to the real woman in front of him, the light playing across her body as she unbuttoned her blouse and dropped it to the floor, keeping her eyes on him the whole time, undoing her jeans and pushing them down, stepping out of them and walking towards him, taking his hand and leading him to the bedroom. He glanced behind at the television, trying to get a glimpse of Maddie before all this happened, but she was gone.

*

'Take me to the boat.'

He was on his back, still breathing hard. She pushed herself up on an elbow and ran a finger down his side to his hip.

He closed his eyes. 'What?'

'The boat at Orphir, I need to get to it.'

Finn didn't open his eyes, just watched the tracers on his eyelids, the light and shade shifting.

Her hand moved up his chest and she pinched his nipple.

'Shit,' he said, flinching and opening his eyes.

'I need to go now,' Maddie said.

He wished he could read people. He stared at her face, her eyes. He didn't have a clue what was going on in her mind. Regret and remorse? Guilt and shame? Self-interest? He couldn't tell if her face was the face of someone scared for her life, desperate to get away from an abusive husband, or the face of a cold-blooded killer. If she had killed Kev, surely she could kill again. Maybe Finn was in more danger than he knew. Or maybe she just felt attracted to him and wanted his help to escape to a new life. Did she even have any feelings towards him?

'What kind of life will you have?' he said.

'What do you mean?'

He sat up in bed and took her hand. He meant the gesture to be kind but he half grabbed it and she narrowed her eyes.

'Say I take you to the boat,' he said, 'and you successfully sail over the firth. Then what? The police are looking for you. You've got no transport, are you going to steal a car? They'll be watching the bus and railway stations. If you get to an airport your passport will be flagged up.'

Maddie sighed. 'Things aren't that connected. Everyone

thinks people in power are competent but they're not, they're as clueless as us. They're not suitable to be in charge any more than we are. Probably less so, because they want to be in charge in the first place.'

'It's unrealistic.'

'What's unrealistic is staying here expecting things to die down before the Lewises come back, or your gran books a tour party. I'm going mad and I've only been here two days. At least if I run I'll be doing something.'

'Those aren't the only options, you know that. You can give yourself up.'

'You're like a broken record,' Maddie said. 'I'll get life in prison. Or worse.'

'What could be worse?'

She gave him the raised eyebrows. 'What you said about the money. If someone killed Kev because he didn't have it, maybe they'll kill again to get it.'

'You think guys are after you?'

'Why not?' Maddie said. 'Everyone else is after me.'

'Do you know who these guys are?'

Maddie thought for a moment. 'Lenny would know.'

'He didn't strike me as the kind of person willing to share information.'

'Exactly my point. He's rotten, the whole thing is rotten. I need to get away.'

Finn felt Maddie staring at him but he didn't turn to her. Every time he looked in her eyes he did what she wanted. He was sick of himself, but he loved it too, loved the baseness of it, the venality, so unlike when he was with Amy. It made him feel alive.

'I'll drive you to the boat,' he said.

She kissed him. 'Thank you.'

'But not right now.'

'Why not?'

'Can you sail it in the dark?'

'There's a torch in the boat.'

'That's ridiculous. We're talking about miles of open water. Do you even know the tides?'

'So when?'

'Tomorrow. I'll check the tides, maritime traffic, weather. I'll put together a backpack of stuff you can use. You'll need to change your appearance when you reach the mainland.'

He almost said 'if', not 'when'.

Then he had a thought. 'Where's the money?'

'Why?'

'Just checking it's safe, that's all.'

'It's safe.'

He thought about the crossing. It was madness, but then this whole thing was madness.

'So where is the boat, exactly? I need to know where I'm going.'

'It's easy to find, turn left off the back road at Orphir, it's signposted Swanbister. At the end of the road, park outside Swanbister House. From there you walk round the bay to the right, there's a small pier at Toy Ness. The *Maddie* is there.'

'The *Maddie*?'

A cloud came over her face. 'He named it after me.'

'Christ.'

'It was a long time ago.'

'And it's remote, no one will see us?'

Maddie shook her head. 'You sometimes get dog walkers on the beach in the bay, but no one at the pier. There are two other boats tied up, but they're for summer fishing. Kev kept the boat there for a reason, he didn't want anyone seeing him going out.'

Finn was silent for a moment. 'So he used to dive in Scapa Flow?'

'With Lenny.'

Finn thought about that. 'You think Lenny killed Kev?'

He was giving her a way out, an alternative story for her to build on.

'Maybe.' She looked at him. 'I was so angry finding him with Claire, I thought she might've done it. But maybe Lenny makes more sense.'

'Or someone else,' Finn said. 'Who did he and Lenny do business with? These other guys.'

'They moved stuff around,' Maddie said. 'I presume drugs.'

'How do you mean?'

'Kev never told me details, but they got a call every now and then, guys with foreign accents. Scandinavian.'

'Smugglers?'

Maddie nodded. 'They'd go out in the boat at night after a call, be gone for hours.'

'They didn't bring stuff back home?'

Maddie shook her head. 'Must've stored it somewhere.'

'Where?'

'Does it matter?'

Finn touched her arm. 'I'm just trying to work out the logistics.'

'Why?'

'Don't you want to know what they were doing?'

'It doesn't make any difference now.'

'There could be drugs hidden out there,' Finn said. 'Maybe only Kev knew where. Maybe Lenny needs to find them. Maybe your foreign friends are after him, I don't know.' He looked around the room. 'And you definitely have the money safe.'

'You already asked me that.'

'Sorry, just nervous. Want to make sure everything's planned out.'

She stood up and pulled on her panties then padded to the toilet.

He looked around the room but didn't see the holdall anywhere.

He got dressed and met her coming out of the toilet.

'I'd better go,' he said. 'Amy is up the road, and Ingrid. Everything has to look normal.'

'You're really going to help me.' Maddie kissed him and squeezed his arm. 'Thank you.'

'Don't thank me yet.'

33

'John Tolbert, Mary Tolbert, Evan Reilly, Brian Dean, Graham Wallace, Stephen McDonald, Derek Drennan, Sean Bayliss.'

His voice was a low murmur, an incantation of the dead. He knelt in the dirt and leaned forward, rubbing his thumbs and forefingers against the order of service in his hands.

'John Tolbert, Mary Tolbert, Evan Reilly, Brian Dean, Graham Wallace, Stephen McDonald, Derek Drennan, Sean Bayliss.'

He began rocking backward and forward. The tomb was freezing cold, his breath billowing out into the raw earth inches from his face. He looked up at the skulls. Only five of them, and now eight names on the dead list in his hands. It wasn't perfect but it would have to do. The skulls stared down at him from through the centuries with empty eye sockets.

He rocked on his haunches until his knuckles were scraping the earth. He held the order of service on the ground and placed his forehead against it.

'John Tolbert, Mary Tolbert, Evan Reilly, Brian Dean, Graham Wallace, Stephen McDonald, Derek Drennan, Sean Bayliss.'

This time from memory, not reading it. It was working, he was absorbing them into his mind, his body, he was keeping them alive in his synapses.

He remembered the widow kicking him in the back as he

lay on the ground. He would find out about her and her dead husband, find out which one he was, everything about him, his hopes and dreams, the little disappointments in his life, the compromises, his secret guilty pleasures, all of it. And he would do the same for all of them. He would dedicate himself to their stalled lives, their brief blips of existence on earth. He would keep their candles flickering in the darkness.

He clutched the order of service and sat up, faced the skulls, his chin raised as he stared back at them and their grimaces.

'John Tolbert, Mary Tolbert, Evan Reilly, Brian Dean, Graham Wallace, Stephen McDonald, Derek Drennan, Sean Bayliss,' he said, louder this time.

*

He slipped into bed next to Amy, his feet freezing. The bedside clock said half three and his mind buzzed. He reached out and touched Amy's back and she muttered under her breath. He could feel grit in his fingernails. He lay on his back and listened to the wind outside, erratic gusts, unpredictable and unknowable.

He'd said he would help Maddie but now, away from her spell, the look in those eyes, her body next to him, he wasn't so sure. If he drove her to the boat he was helping a fugitive. More importantly, he was likely driving her to her death. Taking a boat all the way across the Pentland Firth was insane at any time, let alone winter. If the wind was up she would get blown off course, end up in swells the size of oil tankers. A Polish cargo ship had sunk recently in just a few minutes out there as the wind fought against the tide, the ship hit from all sides.

Maybe he should go with her. But he didn't know any more about boats than she did. Perhaps there was another way to help her escape. In the boot of the car all the way to Stromness, then on to a ferry. But they would be watching the port, and he wasn't allowed off the island. Unless he could somehow persuade Ingrid or Amy to drive, without knowing Maddie was in the boot. No, that was impossible.

Then there was the other option. He didn't have to go along with any of this, he didn't have to help her at all. Just one call to the police and she would be gone from his life. A handful of words down the line to Linklater and Maddie would be taken into custody. Arrested for murder, for evading the police, whatever else they wanted to charge her with for the crash.

Was she capable of stabbing her husband? He tried to picture himself in that situation. Imagined coming home to find Amy being fucked by some big builder or squaddie or firefighter, someone more of a man than him. He pictured the scene in his mind but all he felt was relief. Relief that he didn't have to pretend to love his girlfriend any more. Relief that his own terrible behaviour had been cancelled out. Relief that she'd finally found someone to satisfy her in a way Finn couldn't.

So there it was, he didn't want Amy, he wanted Maddie, and all the shit that came with her. But he couldn't have her either. If he took her to the boat and she somehow got across the sea, what then? He couldn't figure out a happy ending for her, let alone any scenario where the two of them were together. Unless maybe he handed her in to the police and she got off on all charges. So maybe he should give her up for the sake of them both. But she would never forgive him, there was no way round that. And she would never get off anyway, she was right about that. And Amy and Ingrid would know he'd been with her, it would all come out, and his betrayal of his family and girlfriend would be in every newspaper and on every website.

There was no answer. There was no right or wrong. Just different ways of fucking up.

34

'Finn, wake up.'

Ingrid was shaking him. He scrunched his eyes then tried to open them, squinting at her. The room was still dark.

'What time is it?'

'Half eight.'

He'd slept in. Amy wasn't next to him.

'Did you move the car?' Ingrid said.

He pushed up on his elbows. 'What?'

'My car,' Ingrid said. 'Have you been out in it since I went to bed last night?'

'Of course not.'

Ingrid opened the curtains. Still dark out there too, just the purple spread of pre-dawn in the east. 'It's gone.'

'What?'

Ingrid looked at him as if he was stupid. 'It's not there. Someone's taken it.'

Finn rubbed at his eyes. 'Where's Amy?'

'In the kitchen.'

'And she doesn't know anything about it?'

'No.' Ingrid stared out the window. 'Who the hell would steal my car all the way out here?'

Finn shook his head.

Ingrid turned to him. 'When did you get to sleep last night?'

'I don't know. Late.'

'And you didn't hear anything?'

'No.'

'It was outside your window, whoever it was must've started the engine. Are you sure you didn't hear it?'

'I'm sure.'

'How did they get it started?'

'People hotwire cars all the time,' Finn said, immediately regretting his tone.

'Not in Orkney, they don't.' Ingrid headed for the door. 'I'm phoning the police.'

Finn called after her. 'Do you think that's wise?'

Ingrid turned. 'Why wouldn't it be?'

'Just with everything that's gone on,' Finn said. 'Haven't we had enough of the police?'

'My bloody car has been stolen from right outside my house, so I'm going to do something about it. Please get out of bed and help.'

She left the room and Finn rubbed his face.

He grabbed his jeans from the floor and went through the pockets. Ingrid hadn't asked about his spare key but she would soon, or the police would. He went through the pockets again, already knowing the truth. His car key was gone.

He threw his clothes on and lifted his jacket from the peg at the front door. He could hear Ingrid on the phone.

'Finn?' He turned to see Amy in the kitchen, mug of tea in one hand, slice of toast in the other. 'Did Ingrid speak to you?'

'About the car, yeah.'

'Where are you going?' She walked towards him.

'Just outside to take a look around, in case the car's been moved or Ingrid's forgotten where she parked it.'

'She seems convinced it's been stolen.'

'I'm sure she's right, I just want to see for myself.'

She was at him now, sad eyes and furrowed brow. She smelled of shampoo and a familiar crisp perfume. He wanted to touch her but he didn't. He caught the smell of tea from her mug.

'Wrap up,' she said. 'Radio says it's cold out.'

'Sure,' Finn said. 'Back in a minute.'

He lifted the torch from the shelf by the door then silently picked up the spare key to the Tomb of the Eagles van, using his body to shield the action from Amy's gaze. He didn't look back as he left the house.

He stood for a moment where he knew the car had been and looked at the ground. There were patches of gravel, a few potholes and a muddy stretch leading up from the driveway. He examined the mud carefully. No broken glass. He spotted several footprints and put his foot alongside. The prints were a woman's. He scuffed over them, making a mess, then looked around. It was calm, the wind from last night had died. The lighthouses were still blinking across the firth, dawn creeping towards them. He did a slow three-sixty but nothing caught his eye. Over to the west some lights were on in the farmhouse a few miles down the road, people no doubt huddling over a warm breakfast, getting ready for the day's exertions. He looked east, behind Ingrid's cottage, and could make out the roof of the visitor centre. All dark.

He gazed at the building over the rise in the road. He looked back at the cottage, Ingrid and Amy inside. He turned and strode down the road towards the Lewis place, breaking into a run once he was over the bump in the road and out of sight.

Five minutes and he was there. He fumbled for the key and opened the door.

Everything seemed untouched. The visitor centre was as it should be. He ran through to the kitchenette, just a mug on the drying rack. He looked in the bin and saw a handful of teabags.

He tried the connecting door to the Lewis house. Unlocked. He went through into the living room. The spread of Maddie's stuff had all been cleared up, everything back the way it was before. He opened the drinks cabinet. Missing the bottles of gin and brandy they'd drunk together. The glasses were washed and back in place.

In the kitchen, the same, just the empty bottles in the bin.

He went through to the bedroom. The bed was made, her clothes all gone. There was a letter on the bed, a single folded sheet with his name on it:

> Sorry, Finn. I didn't want to leave you, but I don't want you getting in any deeper than you already are. Sorry about Ingrid's car. It'll be where we talked about. I don't know if you ever believed me, but I didn't kill Kev. If I make it, I'll be in touch. I'm sorry you have to face everything alone, about the crash. I know how you feel. We're the same, Finn, we have a connection, I know you feel it. But sometimes that's not enough. Good luck.
>
> Maddie xxx

He crumpled the note into his pocket, then went out the front door and strode over to the car park. It was first light now in the east and the wind was picking up again as he unlocked the Tomb of the Eagles van. The blink of its lights and the beep it gave off made him cringe, as if the eyes of the world were on him. He glanced round then got into the van, started the engine and drove north.

35

The weather closed in fast. Squalls of rain splattered the windscreen and the van rocked as gusts of wind swept in from the west. Down past Sandwick to St Margaret's Hope he could see the chop of the water at high tide out in Scapa Flow. He had a sudden panic that the Churchill barriers would be closed, but as he sped through Cara he couldn't see a police vehicle. He drove on to the first barrier and was hit by a wave arching over the concrete, the wipers unable to cope as water plumed over the van, the wheels skiting on the surface. He braked and steered into the skid, flicking the wipers to full and nudging the van forward. He peered out but nothing was coming the other way. It was stupid driving over the barriers in these conditions, even if the police hadn't closed them yet.

He drove over Burray, then the next barrier, no waves this time, but on the exposed road the wind made the van veer to the right. The next barrier past Glimps Holm was the same, the blockship barely visible in the swells to his right. He came over the hump of Lamb Holm and passed the Italian Chapel, just the final barrier to negotiate. He could see that the road was flooded, and as he looked a big wave dumped itself on to the concrete. The weight of it was enough to crush a car roof and smash in the windscreen. He sat for a moment watching, trying to see a pattern in the waves hammering against the barrier, but it seemed random. He looked behind at the fake stucco front of the Italian Chapel, thought about saying a prayer.

He waited for one more wave to hit up ahead then put the van into gear and revved on to the barrier, his shoulders hunched, neck knotted, hands tight on the wheel as the van threw up spray on either side. The thump of the wipers was a primal drum in his ears, his body tense, waiting for the sea to sweep over him. The van rocked under a gust of wind and spray splashed on the driver's side, then a larger wave swooshed over the bonnet, sounding like rocks hitting the metal. He eased off the accelerator and tapped the brake, then sped up again, forty yards to go, the water on the road shallower now as he emerged on the other side and up the hill away from the barrier, safe on the Mainland.

Finn concentrated on the road in the shitty weather, kept the van steady, the wipers still on full blast. On the outskirts of Kirkwall he took the back road to Orphir, heading past Greenigoe and Hobbister. He didn't pass any other car on the road, everyone had more sense than to be out in this. It was daylight now but you couldn't tell, grey cloud pushing down from above, shrouding everything.

As he got close to Orphir he slowed and squinted, looking for road signs. He saw it, Swanbister, and turned left down a bumpy track full of potholes. The road widened into a dead end and turning place at Swanbister House, just like Maddie said, and he pulled up and killed the engine. The rain hammered on the roof of the van, filling it with noise like gunfire. He couldn't see Ingrid's car anywhere.

He got out and hunched against the weather, turning his collar up for all the good it did. He carried the torch just in case. The waves in the bay were ferocious, swathes of rain sweeping in from the west across the expanse of Scapa Flow. He got to the pier and spotted three boats. The two fishing boats locked down for the season and the third, the *Maddie*, tarpaulin cover still over the deck like it was hibernating for winter. He climbed on board at the back, rain dripping down his neck. Looked around but there was no hint of activity, no sign of Maddie, no sense of anyone having been here.

He glanced round one last time then jogged back to the van. He slumped into the driver's seat and ran a hand through his hair, water spraying over the dashboard and seats. He pulled his phone out of his pocket and called her. The rain still thundered on the roof and the windscreen, so he could only just hear the ringing sound down the line. The phone rang for a long time, fourteen rings, but no voicemail message came on. Eventually it stopped ringing as if she'd answered it, but he didn't hear a voice.

'Maddie?' Finn said.

No reply.

'Are you there?'

He stuck his finger in his ear, trying to drown out the noise of the rain.

'Maddie, say something.'

Nothing.

'You need to speak to me,' Finn said. 'I'm at the boat but you're not here. If you don't tell me where you are, maybe I should call the police.'

She said something but he didn't make it out.

'What?'

'No police.'

'Are you OK?'

'No police.'

'Where are you?'

A long silence again.

'Tell me, Maddie.'

She spoke again but he wasn't sure he heard right.

'Did you say Stromness?'

'Yes.'

'You mean the ferry terminal?'

'No.'

'Then where?'

Another reply, again muffled by the noise in the van. 'What was that?'

'I'm at Claire's.'

Finn wiped a hand down his face and it came away wet.

'I'm on my way.'

She said something else but he couldn't hear clearly. He hung up, threw the phone on the passenger seat and started the engine.

36

The MV *Hamnavoe* was at the pier, a giant lurking behind the gable-end cottages in the murky light. A handful of cars were queuing up to board the ferry as delivery trucks rumbled off the ramp from its gaping maw, headlights slicing the gloom. He took the back way and came down the hill to Claire's place, spotted his gran's car parked across the road and pulled in behind. The rain was heavy but the gusts of wind had subsided a little, which made the rain seem more determined somehow, daggering straight to ground instead of blowing into your face.

He got out and bleeped the van, crossed the road and knocked on the door. He thought about Maddie's voice on the phone, detached or distressed, impossible to tell down the line with the thumping rain. He tried the doorbell, a sing-song chime that felt out of place in this dark, sodden end of the world. He knocked again and waited. Nothing. Eventually he tried the door and it opened.

He was about to shout out but stopped himself. He crept along the hall, rain dripping from his jacket on to the carpet, his feet leaving wet prints. No lights were on and the gloom from outside seeped into the house. He passed a blurry seascape in a cheap frame on the wall, land, sea and sky undifferentiated, all part of the same chaos.

He got to the living room and stopped.

Maddie was sitting on the sofa, hands in her lap, looking into the centre of the room with a vacant stare.

Lying on the floor in front of her was Claire, motionless, curled up as if she had cramp.

The curtains were drawn. Finn's eyes grew accustomed to the half-light and he saw a knife sticking out of Claire's chest. Her hands rested on the end of the handle in a way that could've been trying to push it in or pull it out. Her eyes were open, seeing nothing, and the spread of her blood had taken the shape of an unknown continent on the pale carpet. Her knees were pulled up to her stomach like a baby in the womb and she looked as peaceful as that, nothing could hurt her any more.

Finn knelt down and pressed his fingers to her neck. No pulse, her skin warm. He had no idea how long bodies took to cool down, whether that meant anything.

He looked at the knife. It was a heavy-duty serrated thing, like a farmer or fisherman might have for cutting rope or gutting fish. Not a kitchen knife at all. It seemed out of place in this setting.

'What happened?' Finn said, his eyes on Claire's face. He noticed a smudge of eye shadow. The idea of a corpse wearing make-up made him feel queasy.

Maddie didn't speak, just sat with her head trembling.

Finn turned to her. 'I asked you what happened.' His voice was firm.

The movement of Maddie's head increased. 'I don't know.'

Finn stood up and walked into her eyeline. She lowered her head.

'Don't look away from me,' Finn said. 'Tell me what happened.'

She kept her head down. 'I don't know.'

Finn grabbed her chin and forced her head up.

'What the hell happened here?' he said through his teeth.

She pulled away. 'Don't bully me. I've had that my whole life. I don't need another man who thinks he can boss me about.'

Finn raised his eyebrows. He leaned in, towering over her. 'I've just found you in a room with a dead body. Your supposed best friend. The woman who slept with your husband. I think I deserve an explanation.'

She gave him a defiant look. 'I found her like this.'

Finn put his fingers to the side of his head. 'That's the best you've got?'

'It's the truth, I swear.'

'Swear on what, your best friend's life? Your husband's life? In case you hadn't noticed, they're both dead already.'

'Don't.'

'I've been led around by my dick since day one. You are up to your neck in shit and you've dragged me into it. What for? What did you need me for?'

Maddie looked up at him, big eyes. 'I just liked you.'

Finn laughed. 'Did you like Claire? And Kevin? Because they both ended up with knives in them.'

'I haven't hurt anyone, you have to believe me.'

'I don't have to believe another word you say, it's all bullshit. I feel like the biggest idiot on the planet.'

Finn got his phone out of his pocket. Two missed calls from Ingrid and two from Amy, they were tag-teaming on his whereabouts.

'What are you doing?' Maddie said.

'I'm calling Linklater.'

Maddie got up and put a hand out. 'Wait.'

Finn began pressing numbers. 'No, I've had it up to here with doing what you say. It hasn't exactly done me any good.'

'Please, I'll get charged with murder.'

Finn stared at her.

'You know I didn't do it,' Maddie said.

Finn shook his head. 'All I know is that you leave a trail of bodies behind you.'

Maddie reached for his phone but he pushed her away.

'Are your fingerprints on that knife?' he said, pointing. The sight of Claire made him flinch again.

'No.'

'Then you've nothing to worry about.'

'Why don't we just go?'

Finn nodded sarcastically. 'Good idea, let's leave a crime scene. Again. Because no one could possibly have seen us coming in, like Claire's neighbours. The Tomb of the Eagles van is parked outside with its massive logo. You think anyone will remember that? You think the police might work it out?'

'We can escape together.'

Finn laughed. 'You're deluded. I've done nothing wrong, I don't need to escape.'

Maddie narrowed her eyes. 'What if I say you did it?'

'What?'

'Maybe I came round here and found you over the body, wiping your prints off the knife.'

'Why would I kill Claire?'

'I don't need to answer that,' Maddie said. 'I just need to put doubt in their minds.'

'They wouldn't believe you.'

'They might not, but they might. It would get them off my back for a bit.'

Finn examined her. Still beautiful, even in the middle of all this. Still playing him like she did that first day in the airport lounge. If she threw enough doubt into Linklater's mind he would get sucked in with her. But he'd had enough. Enough scurrying around after her, enough running scared of the police and the press and everyone else. Enough of the whispers and stares in the supermarket, at the memorial, in the pub, everywhere he went.

He looked at the knife sticking out of Claire's chest and imagined pushing it into Maddie. Or himself.

The phone rang in his hand. Amy. He pressed answer with no idea what he would say to her.

'I want the money.' A man's voice, thick Orcadian accent.

'Who is this?'

'I want my money.'

Finn looked around the room for Maddie's holdall.

'Why are you on my girlfriend's phone?'

The man laughed. 'Your girlfriend, that's funny.'

'Where's Amy?'

'She's here.'

'Put her on.'

'She's a little busy at the moment.'

'You'd better not have harmed her.'

'Maybe I have, maybe I haven't. Yet. What are you going to do about it?'

'I'll call the police.'

'I don't think so.'

Finn raised his eyebrows at Maddie, indicating the phone. She just stared at him. 'Why not?'

'Because if you do, I will definitely hurt her.'

Finn ran a hand through his hair. 'Look, who is this?'

'You know who it is.'

Finn looked at Claire's body, blood still oozing from the wound. 'Lenny.'

'Give the boy a fucking prize.'

Maddie's eyes went wide and she shook her head, signalling for him to hang up.

Finn turned away from her. 'Amy has nothing to do with this.'

'But you do, don't you?'

Finn pictured the guy now, crew cut, tattoos, muscles, standard small-town hardman. He looked at Claire's body. Maybe he was more dangerous than that.

'What do you mean?'

'I presume you're with Her Highness.'

Finn looked at Maddie. 'Who?'

'That fucking bitch Maddie.'

'I haven't seen her.'

'Bullshit, you're with her now.'

'I'm not.'

'If you're not with her then she's fucked you over already, just like she did me and Kev.'

'Did you kill Kev?' Finn said.

'I don't know what you're talking about.'

'What happened to Claire?'

'What do you mean?'

'I'm looking at her right now.'

A pause. 'She was fine when I left home.'

'Right.'

Lenny sighed. 'Why not ask your friend Maddie what happened, she might know.'

Finn pinched the bridge of his nose and squeezed his eyes shut, then open again. Floaters darted across his vision.

'Let me speak to Amy,' he said.

'Do you have the two hundred grand?'

Finn looked at Maddie. She'd told him one hundred.

'Let me speak to her.'

Muffled voices on the line. Finn kept his eyes on Maddie. He wondered where the bag was, maybe outside in Ingrid's car, or hidden somewhere else.

'Finn?' Amy was crying, her voice cracked. 'I'm sorry.'

'Are you OK?'

'Don't make a deal with him, he won't stick to it.'

She screamed then sobbed. Finn heard a scuffle.

'Don't hurt her.'

'I'll do whatever I have to,' Lenny said. His voice was more agitated. 'You think I like this? You think I like hurting women? If I don't get the money I'm a dead man. There are bigger things happening than you and your fuckbuddy. I need that money and you're going to get it for me, or your girlfriend and your gran are going to die.'

'Ingrid?'

'Didn't I mention?' Lenny said. 'She's here too. I started on the girlfriend first, thought that would get quicker results, but now I'm thinking that smacking the old bitch might work better.'

'I'll get the money,' Finn said. 'Just leave them alone.'

Maddie was inching towards the door. Finn moved to block her.

'Bring it to me.'

'Where?'

'The Italian Chapel. Half an hour.'

Half an hour was pushing it.

'Bring the money and you can have your family back,' Lenny said. 'If you get the police involved, they die. You know I'm not pissing about.'

He hung up.

Finn put his phone away and looked at Maddie. 'I need the money.'

'It's mine.'

'He's going to kill Amy and Ingrid if he doesn't get it.'

'He's bluffing.' Maddie lowered her head. 'It's all I have.'

Finn gripped her arm. 'You never had it, you never had a chance of getting away with it.'

He pushed his hand into her pocket and felt around.

She tried to pull away. 'What are you doing?'

He went into her other pocket and pulled out the key for the Skoda.

'Give me that,' Maddie said, voice shrill.

'I presume the money's in the car.'

He headed out the front door and across the road in the rain. He could hear her steps behind him. He unlocked the car and looked inside, and there was the bag in the front passenger-seat footwell. He grabbed it, unzipped, and felt through the clothes for the cash at the bottom. It seemed like the same amount as he'd seen before.

He got into the car and threw the bag under his own legs,

put the key in the ignition. The passenger door opened and Maddie climbed in.

'Get out,' Finn said.

'Come on.'

'Get out of the car.'

She gave him a look. 'You were right about the money, of course their lives are more important. Maybe I can help.'

'You've helped enough.'

'I know how Lenny works,' Maddie said. 'I can make sure he sticks to his side of it.'

Finn looked at her for a long time. The engine grumbled and rain thrummed on the car roof. The wipers swished the worst of it away in heartbeats. He shook his head and pulled on his seatbelt.

37

They got stuck behind a truck and a tractor. Finn thumped the steering wheel. The atmosphere in the car was toxic as they crawled over the high ground outside Stromness and down to the Loch of Stenness. Finn darted glances at Maddie but she stared straight ahead. He kept reaching down with his right hand and touching the bag under his knees, tugging on the zip to make sure it was closed. The radio was on low, an incongruous pop station playing top forty hits with a tinny rattle.

Eventually the tractor turned off on to the low road south and they all speeded up.

Finn looked at Maddie.

'Just tell me,' he said.

She turned to look out at the loch. The rain had stopped for now but the surface rippled and chopped, the water a murky grey, a handful of geese and ducks dipping their heads under the surface for food. Finn had always thought these lochs in the centre of the Mainland were the bleakest spot in Orkney. There was something lonely about them, bodies of water cut off forever from the sea by the thinnest strips of haggard land.

'Tell you what?' Maddie said eventually.

'Everything, from the beginning.'

She tucked her hair behind her ear. It could've been flirtatious in other circumstances, but those times had long gone.

'You know,' she said. 'I've told you everything.'

Finn shook his head as he pulled out to overtake the truck. 'I don't know what to believe any more.'

'Believe me.'

She placed her hand on his as he changed gear, another move that might've been suggestive in another life, in a parallel universe where people didn't keep dying around them. Finn imagined Orkney suddenly full of all the people who'd died, all somehow back to life and going about their business, the oil workers heading to their shifts on Flotta, the pilot of the plane arriving home after a hard flight to his wife and young kids.

The song on the radio was an upbeat dance thing, thudding away quietly.

Finn removed his hand from the gearstick, pulling it away from Maddie's grasp.

They passed the large standing stone, traffic slowing as someone up ahead turned for Brodgar and the Stenness Stones. Finn remembered being there the other day, praying for ancient intervention, touching the stones and hoping for something good to happen.

'Did you kill them?' he said.

'No.'

'Did you?'

'No.'

Matter-of-fact, no hysteria. He had to decide what to believe.

They accelerated on to Finstown, more tiny islands out in the bay to the left. Orkney was stupidly beautiful, like God wanted to concentrate all his dramatic views in one small archipelago halfway to the Arctic.

As they approached Kirkwall Maddie fidgeted in her seat

and sat on her hands. Another farm vehicle pulled out in front of them at Quanterness and they slowed. The bend in the road meant Finn couldn't see to overtake. They were doing about twenty miles an hour. Finn stretched his neck and leaned forward, trying to see past the tractor, but they were coming up to the top of the road on a blind bend.

Maddie lunged across Finn and pushed open his door, then she popped his seatbelt buckle, lifted her feet and kicked at his body. Finn jolted to the right and his shoulder smacked into the swinging door, which flew outwards then back in with a crack against his head. He was half out of the seat and clinging to the steering wheel when Maddie gave another two-footed kick and his body shifted. His feet pushed down on the pedals, the engine revving but the clutch full in, the noise ridiculous. He tried to haul himself back into his seat but a third kick sent him banging against the swinging door again, pain through his back and shoulders, knuckles throbbing on the steering wheel as he lost his grip. The seatbelt had released but was tangled in his right arm, stopping him falling on to the tarmac. Maddie tried to prise his fingers from the steering wheel with one hand, pushing at his chest with the other.

'I'm sorry,' she said.

His left hand was off the steering wheel now, just his broken fingers clinging on. The only thing stopping him hitting the road was the seatbelt looped round his shoulder. Maddie tried to haul it free, leaning into him. He grabbed her hair and yanked as hard as he could, heard her scream as she recoiled. He clutched the headrest and pulled himself up, shuffling into the seat and swinging his fist into Maddie's face, catching her hard on the cheek and nose, crunching under his touch. She touched her face, tears in her eyes. He flipped his door shut and popped down the lock then zipped the seatbelt back round, glaring at her then out the windscreen. The car had swerved into the other lane. If anything had been coming the other way he would be dead now, maybe both of them would be. He turned the wheel to sit behind the tractor then threw his foot on the brake until the car stopped.

He sat getting his breath back as Maddie sucked air in through her hands.

He turned to her, shaking.

'Fuck you.'

Maddie took her hand away, touched the trickle of blood from her nose.

'I need to get away,' she said. 'I need that money.'

'So you were going to kill me?'

'We weren't going fast enough. I just wanted you out of the car.'

'People are in danger because of you, and you were going to leave them to die.'

'Lenny won't kill them.'

'You think?' Finn said. 'Either he's a killer or you're a killer. If it's him, he's killed his own wife, so I don't think he'll worry about two strangers.'

Maddie put her hands over her eyes, lowered her head and sobbed.

Finn put the car into gear and headed into Kirkwall, his hands shaking.

On the outskirts he drove past the industrial estate and saw the large sign for the *Orcadian* office. He wondered if Freya was inside typing up her story. He hit the roundabout off the hill and took a right along Pickaquoy Road. It felt bizarre to be driving through town in broad daylight. He imagined everyone he drove past pointing and screaming for him to be stopped and arrested. Across the Peedie Sea he could see the police station where Linklater had questioned him yesterday. Felt like a lifetime ago. How long before Linklater knew about Claire? Finn would turn Maddie in, he knew that, but not now, he still needed her to help with Lenny.

Round the corner from here was the Nordic Studies place where Janet had her office. Finn pictured all these women sitting at their desks tutting at him and how he'd lost control.

He glanced at Maddie and touched the bag under him, rubbed at his rib where the pain was worst, his fingers throbbing in time with his heart. He coughed and blood came into his mouth. He swallowed it, choking as it slid into his belly and burned.

He drove past the supermarket where everyone had stared at him. He had to slow at a pedestrian crossing to let a young mum with a buggy go across. He watched Maddie the whole time.

He turned at Junction Road and thought of the regulars downing drams in the Bothy Bar round the corner. TV crews were probably still hanging around outside St Magnus Cathedral waiting on developments. He imagined driving there now, walking up to someone with a microphone and telling them everything, showing them the bag of money.

Up New Scapa Road he passed the hospital where he stayed the night of the crash. He thought about Sean Bayliss, the argument they'd had. Did it bring on his stroke? He tried to remember the names of the dead that he'd recited last night in the tomb but his mind was too wired to concentrate. So much for keeping their memory alive.

On the southern edge of town he drove past the distillery, imagining the airborne spores from the whisky being sucked into his lungs through the car's air vents.

Then they were out of town and on the familiar road that Finn had driven so many times, places with names like Rashieburn, Nether Button, Gutterpool.

They sped through St Mary's, Finn's pulse in his ears as they got near their destination. The rain had stopped but the wind was gusting in roars. He imagined the wrecks of the blockships rising out of the water and sailing away, their rusted hulls somehow expelling the mass of the oceans.

He slowed the car at the first Churchill Barrier. An Audi was on the causeway forty yards away, roof buckled in, windscreen smashed, wipers sticking up in surrender, the car in a foot of water on the tarmac. As he crawled forward two waves crashed over it. Finn peered out to see if anyone was inside but it was abandoned.

Finn inched past the Audi and then sped up, anxious to get off the barrier before another wave could do the same to the Skoda. He glanced at Maddie, who looked scared, but he didn't know if it was because of the dangerous road or what was to come.

They made it off the barrier. Finn tried to think why Lenny wanted to meet here. There was nothing on Lamb Holm except the Italian Chapel and the low building he'd just passed, the Orkney Wine Company shop. It was closed, of course, like everything. Maybe Lenny wanted the isolation, no witnesses.

The Italian Chapel's white facade glowed like a beacon set

against the murk of the water and the oppressive grey cloud, as if God was shining a light on it. The front of the chapel was concrete but looked like carved stucco, the building just two old Nissen huts bolted together.

A beaten-up jeep was parked outside, no other sign of life. Finn pulled up in the car park and shut off the engine. He looked at Maddie, who held his gaze.

'I'm scared,' she said.

'You need to explain to this maniac why he has to let them go.'

Maddie shook her head. 'I don't want to.'

'I don't give a shit.' He grabbed the holdall, walked round to her side and opened the door. 'Get out.'

38

Finn looked at the blood-red Christ weeping above the door, its features pockmarked by the weather, then he clicked open the door and pushed Maddie inside.

'Finally.' Lenny. The scuffing of feet.

Finn's eyes took a few seconds to get used to the gloom. Ingrid and Amy were sitting on a bench by the wall. The curved walls were covered in painted-on fake brickwork, ornate angels and holy men peering out from starlit heavens on the ceiling. Behind the tiny altar at the far end, a glowing Madonna and child were surrounded by cherubs and priests.

Ingrid had her arm around Amy, their chins raised in defiance. Lenny stood over them holding a gun, an ancient-looking thing like they had in old war movies. It seemed out of place here, a relic, but then Orkney was full of relics.

'You alone?' Lenny said, looking out the window at the barrier.

'Yes.'

'No police?'

'Like you said.'

You could see for miles in all directions and they were surrounded by water, hard to sneak up on. With just the single road, you would spot a police car coming long before they were near.

'What did you bring her for?' Lenny said, nodding at Maddie.

'I didn't have much choice,' Finn said.

He looked at Amy. She had a bruised and swollen eye, dried blood at a cut on her temple, more blood on a tissue in her hand. She stared at Maddie with her good eye and Finn could see her putting it together, all of it.

'Is that her?' Amy said.

Finn nodded.

Maddie pulled away from Finn. 'I haven't done anything wrong.'

Lenny laughed. 'Except take my fucking money.'

'It's my money,' Maddie said.

Lenny raised his chin to Finn, indicating the bag. 'Throw it over.'

Finn looked at Amy and Ingrid. 'Let them go first.'

'Let me spell it out for you,' Lenny said. 'The one with the gun gets to tell the others what to do.'

'You won't use that,' Finn said.

Lenny hauled Amy to her feet and brought the butt of the pistol down on her cheek, splitting the skin, blood spurting on to the thin rug on the floor. Finn stepped forward but Lenny gripped Amy's arm and pushed the barrel of the gun into her neck.

'Don't.'

Finn stopped.

Lenny laughed. 'So your girlfriend came all this way to see you, and you've been shagging that bitch behind her back.'

'Fuck you,' Maddie said.

'I don't blame you,' Lenny said. 'We've all had a good go on Maddie, she wasn't exactly dedicated to Kev. Any chance we got, Kev out the house, me and her were at it like dogs.'

'That's not true,' Maddie said, turning to Finn.

'That's why I was so surprised she went mental at Kev and Claire,' Lenny said. 'What a hypocrite.'

'I didn't,' Maddie said.

'Stabbing your husband to death is fucked up,' Lenny said.

Maddie stared at Lenny. 'You liar, you killed him.'

Lenny put on a confused face. 'Why would I do that? He was my mate and business partner. And business was pretty sweet.'

'Maybe you lost it when you found him with Claire.'

'That slut? I never gave a shit about her.'

'Is that why you killed her?' Finn said.

'What are you on about?' Lenny said.

'Fucking liar,' Maddie shouted. 'Don't twist this round.'

'We just came from your place,' Finn said.

'I found her,' Maddie said. 'You coward.'

'I don't know what you mean,' Lenny said.

Maddie turned to Finn. 'He's lying, I had nothing to do with it, I only took the money.'

Amy stood, blood dripping from her cheek on to her blouse, taking in Maddie.

Ingrid stared at Finn. He turned away from her gaze.

Maddie had her hands out pleading. He remembered her at the airport, putting her belt and shoes back on, swirling the ice in her gin, touching the holdall at her feet.

'Give me the bag,' Lenny said.

Finn shook his head and gripped the bag. 'I need to know what happened.'

Lenny threw a fist into Amy's stomach and she bent over gasping for breath.

'For Christ's sake, Finn,' Ingrid said. Her voice was a jolt to his brain, a flashback to every time she'd told him off over the years, for getting too close to the cliff edge or stepping into the road without looking.

He looked round the room as if searching for an answer then threw the bag at Lenny's feet. Lenny squatted, unzipped the bag and rummaged inside. He smiled and zipped it up again.

'It's all there?'

Finn looked at Maddie. 'Ask her, I've not touched it.'

Maddie nodded.

Lenny slung the bag over his shoulder, stood up and took Amy's arm.

'Good,' he said. 'My friends don't like getting short-changed.'

'Friends?' Finn said.

'What, you're a detective now?' Lenny said.

Finn put out his hands. 'Just let her go.'

Lenny glanced out the window and seemed satisfied there was no one coming along the barrier. Then he looked out the other side to a grassy field, a handful of grazing sheep.

'It's not that simple.'

He looked at his watch, a big thing with a thick metal-link strap. He peered out the window again, this time at the sky.

Finn heard a thin buzz from outside.

Lenny pushed Amy towards the door, the gun pressed into her back.

'We had a deal,' Finn said.

The drone was louder now, the sound of engines.

Finn went to the window and saw a tiny twin-prop plane coming in to land on the field. A couple of sheep shuffled to the corner of the fence as the plane wobbled in, gusts of wind throwing it one way then the other, its nose up in the air as it dropped low over the water out beyond the barrier. The island didn't look big enough for a runway but the plane nudged its wheels on to the grass, flaps up, quick deceleration, then at the other end it turned in a tight arc to face the way it had come.

'Leave Amy, please,' Finn said. 'Take me instead.'

Lenny stared at him. 'She's security. I'll let her go when we land.' He opened the door, looked around then dragged Amy out. 'If any of you leave the chapel I'll shoot her in the face.'

He began to jog across the grass to the plane, dragging Amy with him.

Finn saw her glance backward then stumble as Lenny hauled her along. He dug his phone out of his pocket and threw it to Ingrid. 'Call Linklater, tell her what's happened.'

Ingrid held the phone. 'He said no police.'

'I can't let him take her,' Finn said.

Maddie was at his shoulder. 'Just let them go.'

Finn turned to her. 'You don't get an opinion here.'

He scoped the scene outside. At the other end of the field was a low corrugated-iron building, a farm shed or maybe a small aircraft hangar. The twin-prop was idling a hundred yards from it. From here, Finn could run round the edge of the field, stay low, try to hide behind the fence maybe, make it to the back of the hangar.

Lenny was running across the field to the plane when Amy stumbled and fell, knees in the mud. He pulled her to her feet.

Finn made his decision.

39

He ran across the grass in a low crouch. Lenny was getting started again with Amy, the bag on his shoulder, gun pressed into her side. The plane had its nose pointing along the runway, propellers spinning. Finn ran, chest aching, pain powering through him, pulse pounding. He kept his eyes ahead, fixed on the shed next to the plane. He was hidden by a rise in the grass between himself and Lenny as he thudded on, trainers wet and muddy, legs aching with the strain, head thumping.

Fifty yards, then thirty, then he was there at the shed. He ran to the far side and came round behind the plane. The engines were going full blast, the roar of the propellers reminding him of the Loganair flight. He remembered the throb of the cabin as they took off, the constant rattle, a tin can hurtling through the sky. This plane was smaller than the Loganair one, maybe just a four-seater. He wondered where it had come from. Maddie said Kev and Lenny had Scandinavian friends. Could it have come across the North Sea?

Lenny and Amy were fifty yards away from the plane, the cabin door still closed. She stumbled again. Lenny yanked her arm and glanced back at the chapel. No sign of movement there.

Finn looked around for something he could use. Along the wall of the shed was a pile of mossy rocks. He examined them, picked one that fitted in his palm and had an edge to it. Lenny and Amy were twenty yards from the plane now, the air filled with noise, sheep cowering in the corner of the field, bunched up against the barbed-wire fence.

Finn ran towards the plane, the stone in his hand.

Lenny reached the aircraft door and hauled it open. He looked back at the chapel, and Finn wondered if Ingrid had got hold of Linklater yet. He kept running as Lenny shoved Amy into the opening, pushing as she protested. The gun in his hand was pointing out wide as he used his palms to force her inside. Finn was just thirty yards away now, the propellers screaming. Lenny slung the bag off his shoulder and into the plane, then put his hands on the doorframe and pulled himself up.

Finn was almost at the plane when Lenny reached out to grab the door and close it. He saw Finn coming at him, a look of surprise on his face as he raised the gun and pointed it at Finn's face.

Finn launched the stone at Lenny and it connected with his forehead, knocking him off balance as Finn reached the doorway. He got hold of Lenny's legs and pulled, got a kick in the face as Lenny lost his footing and landed on his back. Lenny kicked Finn in the face again, harder this time. Finn fell back and looked up and Lenny had the gun back on him. He threw himself forward and landed on top of Lenny in the cabin, their legs hanging out the door as the plane began to move, slowly at first, then picking up speed. Finn grabbed Lenny's gun hand and pushed it away, then heard a pop and felt a burning sensation in the meat of his thumb. He tried to swing the gun round but Lenny was stronger and brought the barrel down on the back of Finn's head. Finn felt sick. He saw Lenny's face in front of him and felt his nose burst under the force of a headbutt. His grip on the gun loosened and he felt the handle of it against the back of his head.

A knee in his chest and the pain roared through him. He was close to letting go, no strength in his arms or legs, one more shove and Lenny would be free, leaving Finn on the grass with the plane halfway across the field. The twin-prop was faster now, the air rushing past as Finn held Lenny's neck in a weak grip. Lenny brought the gun round and pointed it in Finn's face. Behind them, Amy picked up the rock Finn had thrown and brought it down on the back of Lenny's head.

He fell forward into Finn, almost pushing him out of the plane, the gun falling from his hand and spinning out of the plane door. Finn put a hand on the doorway to steady himself but Lenny recovered and stuck the heel of his boot into Finn's chest. He pushed with his foot, Finn grabbing the other side of the doorframe to keep himself inside, but his grip was slipping. He saw Amy behind Lenny again, this time with a piece of rope that she looped around his neck and yanked, the two of them tumbling backward into the cabin.

Finn hauled himself inside and tried to get off his knees but his legs were unsteady. Lenny scrambled at the rope and got it off his neck then turned and punched Amy in the face, her head jerking back and thunking off the cabin wall. Finn threw himself at Lenny as he tried to get up, the pair of them jostling and landing on the passenger seats behind the cockpit. The pilot looked round and shouted something Finn couldn't hear over the rush of the engines.

'Get off,' Finn yelled to Amy, nodding at the open door.

Amy hesitated then got up and ran to the cabin door but

they were already moving too fast, the grass outside a blur.

Lenny got a hand free and punched Finn in the face. Finn tasted blood and spat at Lenny, who shrank back and wiped his eyes. Finn threw a fist into Lenny's guts, the bones in his hand screaming. Lenny doubled over and looked confused, first at Finn then down at his stomach. Finn looked at his hand and saw blood on the metal splint running along the outside of his knuckle.

He punched Lenny in the face with his other hand. He got up to kick him but felt a crack on the back of his skull and stumbled forward.

He turned and saw the pilot still in his seat. He was in his forties, messy beard and a biker jacket, and he was clutching a wrench in his fist. Finn touched the back of his scalp and his hand came away red. His eyes were full of tears and sparks of light. He lunged at the pilot and grabbed the wrench. The pilot was trying to pull the controls up. Out the cockpit window the sea was approaching fast, they were running out of grass before they'd plunge into the water. Finn sank his teeth into the pilot's hand and grabbed the wrench, then turned and saw Lenny staggering towards him. Behind him, Amy was bracing herself against the roof of the cabin as the plane bumped across the field. Finn swung the wrench at Lenny's face and caught him square on the jaw, the bone collapsing as his head jerked sideways and he fell to his knees. Finn swung the wrench again and landed it on the side of Lenny's head above the ear, blood spraying out the wound, the skin splitting to show pink bone underneath.

The plane lurched sideways as the pilot hauled at the controls and lifted the nose a few feet off the ground, but it was lopsided, the right wing higher than the left. Finn fell into the co-pilot's seat. Lenny slumped to the floor, clutching the side of his head. Amy stood over him, staring at the grey swells of the North Sea fifty yards away.

'Strap in,' Finn shouted, nodding at the seats behind her.

She staggered backward and scrambled to click the seatbelt around her waist. Finn did the same thing in the co-pilot's seat, fumbling with the belt as the loose set of controls in front of him jerked around, the pitch and yaw of them mirroring the pilot's moves.

The roar of the engine and the landing gear was joined by successive bangs as the cabin door flapped and slammed against the body of the plane. The pilot gave the controls a final wrench to take the plane off the ground. There were twenty yards of grass left sloping down to a thin rocky shore, two sheep scuttling to the side petrified by the noise, the wheels still rattling on the ground, the nose dipping for a second so that they were aiming straight for the rocks, then they pitched up to the horizon, wavered for a moment then climbed higher, the wheels lifting off the grass just as it ran out under them, the engine whining as they took to the air.

The right wing rolled upwards until they were at forty-five degrees to the horizon, Finn slung over in his seat, the controls battering his knees as they span and twisted, the pilot swearing in a foreign language as he grappled with the stick. The plane made a sickening upwards lurch, then another stagger to the left and down, turning too sharply back towards Lamb Holm. They thrust forward along the coastline, still at a terrible angle to the ground, the wings rolling one way then the other, then yawing to the left so that they rushed past the Italian Chapel, the rocks of the beach underneath, then a flip back and they were pitching nose first towards the Churchill Barrier.

Finn heard a noise with the last lurch and looked round. Lenny's body was flipped over, ten yards behind Amy, lying like a discarded toy. Amy's hands were on the armrests, eyes wide, neck muscles straining. The pilot had deep furrows in his brow, panic in his eyes. The plane took a shrug upwards, a dying effort, then pitched left and down, flipping almost upside down as the pilot fought with the controls. Finn was aware of the sea at the edge of his vision, then there was an almighty crash and he realised their left wing had hit the water, flipping the plane. A sickening whump and jolt as the fuselage hit the water and the cockpit window shattered, Finn raising his arms to cover his face, broken glass on his skin, a chunk of something battering his shoulder as he was thrown forward by the deceleration, then the shock of the icy water pouring over him as he struggled to breathe.

The plane was sinking fast. The shock of the cold hammered Finn's lungs. The pilot was gone, Finn couldn't see where. He unbuckled his belt, turned and saw Amy slumped in her seat, eyes closed, head to the side. He staggered over as the water in the cabin rose to his knees, then up to his waist in no time. He fumbled at the release on her belt under the water, his hands numb. He released the catch and grabbed under her arms, dragged her into the cockpit, the water already at his chest, then with his arms locked around her he pushed out the empty cockpit window frame, water surrounding him. He got outside and found his feet touching the nose of the plane. He kicked against it, coldness tight in his body, the weight of Amy pushing down on him, the force of the water trying to crush him. He kicked towards the surface, grey all around, seaweed clutching his legs in the murk.

He broke the surface with a gasp, heaving in breath, coughing up water and blood, salt in his mouth. Amy was still limp. He looked round, treading water. Lamb Holm was two hundred yards to his left. The barrier was the same distance in front of him. He looked behind and saw an orange buoy, the kind they use to mark lobster pots, only thirty yards away. He was no great swimmer, he could do two hundred yards in a calm, heated pool, but not here. He headed for the buoy though it felt counter-intuitive, swimming away from land. He kicked and paddled on his back, Amy across his chest, the cold seeping into his bones. He kept pushing and was surprised that after a few minutes he was at the buoy. He threw one arm around the rough plastic and heaved Amy's weight closer to him with the other.

His body shook as he looked around. He knew where the plane had hit the water, but already there was no sign of it. He scanned the choppy surface and spotted someone swimming towards the beach. Looked like the pilot.

No sign of Lenny.

He turned to the island. A handful of figures stood at the Italian Chapel, stark against the building. In the car park were three police cars and an ambulance, lights flashing.

He shouted in their direction.

40

Linklater looked up from her notebook. She seemed worn through, skin pale and stretched, hair in a greasy ponytail. Finn wondered how he looked to her, with all his injuries. He straightened his back and cricked his neck, blades of pain slicing through him. He took shallow, careful breaths and tried not to upset the equilibrium of his body.

'I did warn you,' Linklater said.

They were back at the police station, this time with the official tape going and the jowly cop in tow. Linklater sighed. She'd asked him to finally tell the truth, and for the last hour he had, all of it, all that he could remember anyway. He'd hoped his injuries might buy him a day or two in hospital, put off this little chat. But the ambulance crew at the scene saw to his cuts and bruises, and the superficial gunshot wound to his thumb, and he was deemed fit for interview.

Amy was in hospital. A police dinghy had picked the two of them up from the buoy after a few minutes. Some paramedics scurried around her for a while, then she was taken to the Balfour. According to Linklater she was awake and had no serious injuries. Concussion, the damage from Lenny's beatings, but very lucky.

The police also picked up the pilot, a Norwegian called Gunnar according to his wallet. He refused to speak without a lawyer, but they'd been in touch with Norwegian police and he was known to them, had spent time in prison for drug-smuggling out of a fjord south of Tromsø.

Finn waived his right to a solicitor, which was maybe why Linklater cut him some slack and filled him in about the others. Police divers were in Holm Sound examining the wrecked plane, trying to find Lenny. Another officer was taking a statement from Ingrid.

Maddie was gone.

Finn grabbed a few words with Ingrid while he was being treated in the ambulance and she told him that Maddie had bolted just after Finn left the chapel, taking Ingrid's car. Finn checked his pocket and sure enough, his car key was missing. He told Linklater to check the boat in Orphir. They sent an officer, who found Ingrid's car parked with the key still in it, the boat gone. The coastguard was scrambled. They were still searching, but had found no sign of her. Maybe she really sailed across the Pentland Firth. Maybe she even made it. Then what?

Maybe she hadn't gone across the firth at all, but hid the boat somewhere along the coast to throw them off, then doubled back and got the ferry. The cops were looking for her there too so she couldn't just walk up, but there were plenty of delivery trucks she could hide inside, maybe sweet-talk a driver into keeping her out of sight.

Finn was relieved to be telling the truth. How she flirted with him, how she walked away from the crash. How she called him and he went running, doing as she asked, hiding her, screwing her. How he betrayed Amy and lied to Ingrid.

He wasn't in the clear about the murders yet. They had various DNA samples from the two murder scenes, but nothing so far that matched the swab they took from Finn. That didn't mean anything, of course, what they needed was a positive match to Lenny or Maddie. But Lenny was on the seabed somewhere and Maddie was AWOL. Even if they got a match it might not be conclusive, Linklater said, given that the two murder scenes were Maddie and Lenny's homes anyway.

He thought about the bag of money, presumably still in the Norwegian plane.

He thought about Lenny and Maddie. He told Linklater what they each said in the chapel, that the other one committed the murders.

'Indulge me,' Linklater said, arms spread. 'What do you think happened?'

Finn thought for a long time.

'I think Lenny killed Kev,' he said.

'Why?'

'I don't know. Either because of Kev and Claire or the money. Maybe both.'

'And you think he killed Claire too?'

Finn nodded.

'Why?'

'Maybe she knew he killed Kev. She seemed scared when I met her. Or maybe he thought she knew where the money was. Tried to get it out of her but it went too far.'

Linklater pursed her lips. 'So you still don't think Maddie had anything to do with the murders?'

Finn pictured her kicking at him, trying to push him out of the moving car. He pictured her unbuttoning her blouse in the Lewis place, leading him to the bedroom.

'No.'

'We'll see,' Linklater said. 'Where do you think she is now?'

'Your guess is as good as mine.'

There was silence between them for a time.

'You stepped into a real nest of snakes, didn't you?' Linklater said.

Finn just looked at her.

Linklater flicked the pages of her notebook back and forth. Eventually she looked up, and Finn wondered if he saw sympathy in her eyes.

'For now, I'm willing to believe you didn't kill Kevin Pierce or Claire Buchan. Though the evidence might prove otherwise.'

'Thanks.'

She waved a hand in front of her. 'But the rest of this. Perverting the course of justice, obstructing an investigation, aiding and abetting a wanted suspect, possibly assisting a murder.'

'I never did that.'

'And that's not even including the plane crash,' Linklater said. 'I mean the first plane crash. Depending on the powers that be, that could be terrorist charges.'

'I'm not a terrorist.'

'It's out of my hands.'

'Couldn't you put in a word for me?'

Linklater stared. 'Why would I do that?'

'You know I'm not a bad person.'

Linklater shook her head. 'I don't know anything of the sort.' She looked at her watch. 'I need a break. Interview terminated at four thirty-five pm.' She reached over and pressed stop on the recording device.

'You are a fucking idiot,' she said. 'You know that.'

'Yeah.'

Linklater nodded at the door. 'Get some fresh air, it could be your last chance for a long time.'

41

He went to the toilet in the police station and splashed water on his face. He looked in the mirror. He remembered looking in the mirror of the toilet on the plane, squinting at his fuzzy image, thinking about Maddie, talking to Amy on the phone. All the deception started there, but he'd been deceiving Amy long before that, lying to her about how he felt. Maddie was an excuse.

The door opened and Freya from the *Orcadian* breezed in.

'This is the men's toilet,' he said.

'I should hope so, I'd hate to find you in the ladies'. Add it to your long list of indiscretions.'

'That's a nice way of putting it.'

'Isn't it?'

'Is that how you'll write it up?'

She leaned her head to one side. 'I might use a slightly more serious tone, given the nature of your situation.'

'I'm completely innocent.'

'I'm sure you are.' She lifted a digital recorder out of her pocket. 'Why don't you tell me about it?'

Finn looked beyond her at the door. 'How did you get in here?'

'It pays to have local knowledge,' she said, tapping her nose. 'My cousin is a cleaner here.'

'Everyone knows everyone else's business on these islands, don't they?'

'You say that, yet we've had murders and affairs and plane crashes and fugitives on the run and God knows what else, and no one seemed to know a thing about it.'

She lifted the recorder and touched his arm.

'So, my story?'

Finn looked at her for a long time.

'OK.'

42

He stood outside the Centre for Nordic Studies and stared at the longship. He pushed the door open and the receptionist looked startled. He walked to Janet's office and knocked twice.

'Come.'

He poked his head in the door.

She smiled when she saw him.

'Do you have a minute?' Finn said.

She waved him in. He slumped in the seat opposite her desk, met her gaze, then closed his eyes. He just wanted to sleep. He listened to the silence, tried to feel empty. But the thoughts kept coming, replaying in his mind. The lurch in his stomach as the plane plummeted through the fog, the look in Maddie's eyes in the departure lounge, the skulls at the Tomb of the Eagles lining up to judge him, Claire's hands clutching at the knife handle, the feel of the standing stones under his fingers in the sleet. Amy's face when she knew what he'd been up to with Maddie, the emergency vehicles and their blinking lights, the dead oil workers, that couple sliced up in the front seats, the investigators crawling over the wreckage, the plane like a corpse on the runway, the gin on Maddie's breath, the taste of her skin.

'How are you?' Janet said.

He tried to take a deep breath to quell the panic. He felt like his blood was dying, not enough oxygen, and he put his hands on the armrests of the chair to feel something solid, to attach himself to the room.

'I've been better.'

Silence for a few more moments, Finn's eyes still closed. Eventually he opened them and looked at her. She had a kind smile and worried eyes. He'd seen that combination a lot over the last few days, from so many people.

Janet spoke. 'Everything you've been through, there are mitigating circumstances. You know that.'

Finn shook his head. Of course Janet had spoken to Ingrid.

Janet leaned forward. 'Survivor guilt. Post-traumatic stress.'

'Not good enough,' Finn said. 'Those are excuses.'

'I don't believe you're a bad person, Finn.'

He snorted with laughter. 'I wish I shared your confidence.' He looked at the flag on the wall, then out the window. 'People are defined by their actions and my actions have been terrible.'

'Maybe people are defined by their intentions.'

Finn rubbed at his forehead, then his knuckle. 'Maybe my intentions weren't any better than my actions.'

'I don't believe that.'

Finn smiled and looked her in the eye. 'Can I come and see you again, just to talk?'

'Of course.'

'If I'm not in prison, I mean.'

Janet put her hands flat on the desk.

'I'm not going anywhere.'

43

Squalls of rain swept across the sky, patches of light and shade dappling the sea like drifting islands. Mainland Scotland sat in the distance like a thick steak, the gristle of Stroma and the Skerries in between. It looked impossible to get across this stretch of water in a tiny boat. Finn tried to imagine being out there, swamped by waves, the prow flipping into the air with each swell, crashing back down into the troughs, hoping every moment not to go under.

Twenty-four hours and the coastguard still hadn't found anything. Police were patrolling the mainland, but there was too much coastline. It came down to that, the vastness of the land, the smallness of a single person, so easy to disappear.

Divers had retrieved Lenny's body, which had gone for autopsy and forensic tests. Finn wondered if it would come back that he drowned, or maybe that he was dead already. All those injuries on his body. Finn looked at the splint on his hand, ran a finger along the sharp metal edge.

There was no sign of the holdall in the plane wreckage. It could've been thrown clear, of course, or taken by currents. He gave that some thought.

He heard footsteps and turned to see Ingrid coming towards him from the cottage, a newspaper in her hand. As she got closer, he saw it was the *Orcadian*. They'd run a special edition full of Finn. Freya texted him first thing this morning to say thanks, she already had national papers offering jobs.

'Want to see it?' Ingrid said, holding the paper out. She had a cup of tea in her other hand, the steam from it whipped away by the wind.

Finn shook his head and looked out at the Pentland Firth.

Amy was gone. She'd spent the night in the Balfour, then left on the first flight to Edinburgh. Finn imagined her on the plane, the same kind of Loganair junk he'd been in. She'd refused to see him or talk to him, and he was relieved about that. He had no excuses. He'd treated her so badly and had almost got her killed. She deserved better. She'd told Ingrid she would move out of the Perth Road flat but Finn said to tell her that she could stay as long as she liked. He wouldn't be back any time soon, given that he couldn't leave the islands.

Somehow Ingrid had arranged bail, on the understanding that he stayed with her. They didn't consider him a flight risk, the irony of that phrase, and besides, how would he get off the island without being caught?

He'd spent the last twenty-four hours apologising to her. He didn't know if he would ever stop apologising. She got so sick of him saying sorry that she made him go outside and get some air. So here he was, all the air in the world, and it didn't make a bit of difference.

'You forget,' Ingrid said. 'Living here, I mean. You sometimes take all this for granted.'

'Yeah.'

'You can see why the old guys up the road lived here in the first place, can't you?'

Five thousand years of living here at the end of the earth. Men and women just staying alive, keeping the species going, no purpose other than living the best life they could. There was banal heroism in that, glory in just eating and drinking and shitting and pissing, laughing and crying and screwing and fighting. And dying. Doing it together because that's what we've always done, trying to make it to the end without too much drama.

Finn had had his fill of drama. And yet all the consequences were still to come.

He thought about what he'd told Linklater, that he believed Lenny was the murderer, not Maddie. Did he really believe that? He'd thrown it around in his mind ever since, picking at it constantly. He had to believe it, he just had to, otherwise what kind of an idiot did it make him, that he was played so easily?

He felt Ingrid's hand on his shoulder.

'I'm sorry,' he said for the millionth time.

She left her hand there. 'I know.'

A rain shower from the west had reached them now, the first freezing spots on his face.

'Why don't you come inside,' Ingrid said.

'In a second.'

He listened to her footsteps on the gravel and waited to hear the cottage door open then close. Still looking out to sea, he pulled his phone out of his pocket. He stood feeling the weight of it in his hand for a moment, then opened his messages. There was the text he'd received an hour ago, from a number he didn't recognise.

I made it. x

He rubbed his thumb across the screen and smiled, then raised his face to the cold rain, felt it sting his skin.

Acknowledgements

Huge thanks to my editor Angus Cargill and everyone else at Faber & Faber for their continued enthusiasm and support – Sophie Portas, Lisa India Baker, Lizzie Bishop, Eleanor Rees, Alex Kirby, Miles Poynton, Lee Brackstone, Hannah Griffiths and Samantha Matthews. Thanks to my agent Phil Patterson and author Alison Miller for invaluable feedback. And big thanks to Tricia, Aidan and Amber for inspiration.

Also by Doug Johnstone

The Jump

What if you got a second chance?

Struggling to come to terms with the suicide of her teenage son, Ellie lives in the shadows of the Forth Road Bridge, lingering on its footpaths and swimming in the waters below. One day she talks down another suicidal teenager, Sam, and sees for herself a shot at redemption, the chance to atone for her son's death. But Sam's troubled family has some dark secrets of its own, and even with the best intentions, she can't foresee the situation she's falling headlong into.

From the number-one-bestselling author of *Gone Again*, *The Jump* is a hugely moving contemporary thriller, and a stunning portrait of an unlikely heroine.

'A brilliant psychological thriller, no, domestic noir, whatever you call it, *The Jump* is superb.' **Helen Fitzgerald**

'His darkest, heaviest and most heart-wrenching piece of work yet. Very serious stuff but beautifully done.' **Irvine Welsh**

ff

The Dead Beat

If you're so special, why aren't you dead?

The first day of your new job – what could possibly go wrong?

Meet Martha.

It's her first day as an intern at Edinburgh's *The Standard*.

Put straight onto the obituary page, she takes a call from a former employee who seems to commit suicide while on the phone, something which echoes events from her own troubled past.

Setting in motion a frantic race around modern-day Edinburgh, *The Dead Beat* traces Martha's desperate search for answers to the dark mystery of her parents' past. Doug Johnstone's latest page-turner is a wild ride of a thriller.

'Riveting. Fearless. Twisted. If Tartan Noir was a family with an irreverent rebel child, his name would be Doug Johnstone.' *Daily Record*

'There's a tangible sense of expectation and excitement to this rollercoaster tale of dark secrets.' *Lancashire Evening Post*

'A twist-laden tale of family secrets.' **Howard Calvert**, *Mr Hyde*

ff

Gone Again

A missing wife –
A father and son left behind

As we learn some of the painful secrets of Mark and Lauren's past – not least that this isn't the first time Lauren has disappeared – we see a father trying to care for his son, as he struggles with the mystery of what happened to his wife . . .

'A major discovery.' *Spinetingler*

'Excellent . . . sharp and moving.' *The Times*

'Calling to mind the best of Harlan Coben, Johnstone shows us how quickly an ordinary life can take one dark turn and nothing is ever the same again.' **Megan Abbott**, author of *Dare Me* and *The End of Everything*

'Deeply poignant and compelling . . . it's hard to take your eyes off the page.' *Daily Mail*

'Riveting from start to finish.' *The Skinny*

ff

Hit & Run

The worst night of your life just got worse . . .

High above Edinburgh, on the way home from a party with his girlfriend and his brother, Billy Blackmore accidentally hits a stranger.

In a panic, they drive off.

The next day Billy, a journalist, finds he has been assigned to cover the story for the local paper.

'A great slice of noir.' **Ian Rankin**

'This noirish crime novel builds into something more substantial: an existential thriller where a man crumbles as he tries to scream the truth in a house of liars. Thus *Hit & Run* becomes a grisly parable for our times.' **Irvine Welsh**

'With this book, Doug Johnstone hits YOU and then HE runs, and you never catch him until the last word of the last sentence on the last page. Cracking stuff.'
Alan Glynn, author of *Graveland*

'Fantastic: sparse and fast-paced but believable and emotionally satisfying. You feel you could be Billy – and you thank God you're not. His best yet.' **Helen FitzGerald**, author of *The Cry*

ff

Smokeheads

Four friends. One weekend. Gallons of whisky.
What could go wrong?

Four friends, spurred on by whisky-nut Adam, head for a weekend to a remote Scottish island, world famous for its single malts. They have a wallet full of cash, a stash of coke, and a serious thirst. Determined to have a good time and to relive their university years, they start making friends: young divorcee Molly, whom Adam has a soft spot for, her little sister Ash, who has all sorts of problems, and Molly's ex-husband Joe, a control freak who also happens to be the local police.

But events start to spiral out of control and soon they are thrown into a nightmare that gets worse at every turn . . .

'It lulls the reader with the warm glow of a good dram on a winter's night, then ambushes him with all the bitter nastiness of a brutal whisky hangover.' **Christopher Brookmyre**

'A hugely atmospheric thriller soaked in the spirit of life . . . sip and savour.' *The Times*

'It is so well written . . . there is plenty of flesh and blood here, much of it splashing across the page.' *Scotsman*